HOOP CITY
WASHINGTON, D.C.

SAM MOUSSAVI

EPIC
Press

Washington, D.C.
Hoop City: Book #5

Written by Sam Moussavi

Copyright © 2016 by Abdo Consulting Group, Inc.

Published by EPIC Press™
PO Box 398166
Minneapolis, MN 55439

Cover design by Nicole Ramsay
Images for cover art obtained from Shutterstock.com
Edited by Lisa Owens

Library of Congress Cataloging-in-Publication Data

Moussavi, Sam.
Washington, D.C. / Sam Moussavi.
p. cm. — (Hoop city)
Summary: When "Hoop City" High head coach Tony Wilson gets cancer, Julius
Dunbar, an unknown in coaching circles, is chosen by the athletic director to take
over the team. Can coach Dunbar carry on Coach Wilson's legacy and write a new
chapter in the school's rich history?
ISBN 978-1-68076-048-4 (hardcover)
1. Basketball—Fiction. 2. High schools—Fiction. 3. Inner cities—Fiction.
4. Teamwork—Fiction. 5. Young adult fiction. I. Title.
[Fic]—dc23
2015903978

EPICPRESS.COM

To Marina, with a white butterfly fluttering just above her shoulder

ONE

People talk about how wild these kids are, how they don't listen. People said I wouldn't be able to get through to them because of my past. They said I was too much like them because I came from the same place.

Shit, *I* was still a kid then.

———

"I want you to do this, Julius," Coach Wilson said. "I'm not going to let you refuse it."

"Coach, you've been like a father to me," I said. "You've taught me a lot, and not just about basketball. I think you are one of the smartest men I know. But I don't think you are right about this."

Coach Wilson's hair was starting to fall out from the chemo. When I saw him the year before, his hair was full of those black curls that made up half of his classic look. The other half came from the way he dressed on the sidelines—suits, always suits. Now his outfits were made up of hospital gowns and nothing else. The cancer came out of nowhere and it was aggressive, like a star player who knows that the defender in front of him is overmatched.

Chemo was the last hope.

"I'm right about this," he said. "I can feel it right here."

Coach Wilson pounded his heart softly with a balled first.

It was hard sitting there with him, seeing him reclined in that hospital bed and not even able to stand for more than five minutes. It was tough seeing him like that because only five years earlier, when I played for him on the varsity team at Dunbar High School, he was fit enough to run up and down the floor with us. He would school us every once in a while with his "old man game," filled with pump fakes, jab-steps, and solid footwork.

"Let's say I took the job," I said. "Why would Dunbar want someone with no experience coaching on the high school level?"

He didn't say anything; he just stared at me lazily.

"And also, I'm sure they haven't forgotten what happened during my junior year," I said. "I mean, how could they?"

His eyes appeared tired—there was no other way to describe them. They sagged and then slowly re-opened with every short breath. I felt bad sitting there and sapping the little energy he had left.

"Son," he said, "time is the great solver of problems."

He licked his lips but they still looked dry and brittle.

"It can untangle the most complicated situation," he said. "But that's not the real issue here. You need to forgive yourself first."

I didn't say anything. I just stared at him. The feeling of respect that I had for him would never go away. I didn't want to say goodbye to him, but I knew he needed his rest.

"You gotta let it go, Julius," he said. "Everyone else has."

"Okay Coach," I said as I stood up and gave him a hug.

His body was frail. What was once a strong and sturdy man filled with energy and a love of life, particularly for things that revolved around the game he loved, was now a thin, brittle shell of a man. It broke my heart. "Get some sleep, okay?" I said as I patted his hand.

"Come see me tomorrow, Julius," he said with his eyes closed. "I'm not going to stop until you take the job."

I smiled but he didn't see it. He fell asleep, and before I left I watched his chest rise and fall a few times. I wanted to make sure that it wasn't over, that I would get a chance to see him the next day.

TWO

From the time I was young, the streets of Washington, D.C., were where I felt most comfortable. I didn't have a father, which was typical for where I grew up. My mother was there, but not really. She didn't work or do much of anything.

We moved a lot because she didn't work. Every two years or so, my mother, two brothers, and I would pack up the little that we had and move it to some other place that looked just like the other places before it. Shortly after moving in, my brothers and I would be out the door exploring our new neighborhood, finding out what was what, who was who, and understanding how to survive it all.

The streets raised my brothers and me. I was the youngest, constantly looking up to my two big brothers. John was the oldest and Myron was the middle child. The three of us were tight. John and Myron always looked after me, whether it was in one of the little scrapes in the neighborhood or the big ones. But as we all got older, things got more serious. Soon, my brothers were out on the corner all night, and with that came *the life*. It was a life that a lot of young males in D.C. were choosing and still to this day choose. They started selling crack.

It didn't end well for my two brothers. They were killed when I was a junior at Dunbar, both shot dead because of the game and all that came with it. John went first, and soon thereafter, Myron. The night that John died changed my life. It sent me down the path that John never wanted for me. I'll never forget it. One minute you're one place, the next minute you're somewhere else. That's how I felt growing up with my two brothers in D.C.

Before he died, John hoped that my life would be different from his and Myron's because of basketball. It didn't work out that way though. I spent two-and-a-half years in jail for being involved with a murder.

———

I went to see Coach Wilson again the day after. He didn't look any better—I don't know why I expected him to after another round of chemo—but he did at least look more alert.

I gave him a hug like I always did and sat down next to his bed.

He was a father figure to me and to countless other kids who grew up on the streets of D.C. without a father. John tried to fill that void, but how could he? He was only five years older than me. I didn't even know what it meant to have a relationship—a real relationship—with an older male until Coach Wilson came into my life.

"What do you say, Julius?" Coach Wilson asked, skipping the small talk and coming right out with it.

"Coach, I'm too young to be head coach of a major high school basketball program," I said. "I'm only turning twenty-one next month."

I knew Coach Wilson. He wasn't going to give up until I agreed to take the job.

The only coaching experience I had at the time was with the Boys & Girls Club in my old neighborhood in Anacostia. This was after I was released from jail. I was at a practice with my ten-year-old boys' team when Coach Wilson first sent word to me about the job at Dunbar. That was just after he got sick.

"Why me, Coach?" I asked. "You know everyone in this city. Shit, you know the best and most experienced basketball people in D.C., Maryland, and Virginia. Why would you think of me to take over for you?"

He smiled and shook his head like I imagined a father would to his young and inexperienced son.

"There are so many people in this area who are more qualified for this job than me," I said. "I don't deserve it."

Coach Wilson sat up in his bed the best he could. His skin was pale and it clashed with the sunlight that sprayed into the room.

"You've been through something, Julius," he said. "And you come from where they come from."

"I hear you, Coach, but—"

"You're not *hearing* me," he said. "You can teach these kids something."

I didn't say anything.

"Just give Josh a call," he said with a smile and a chin nod. "Today or the next day."

Josh Allen was the athletic director at Dunbar High. He was highly respected in the D.C. area.

I thought about it for a moment while Coach stared back at me. I had fifty good reasons why I wasn't right for the job, but I couldn't answer the look in Coach's eyes. Something in them told me that he was right. Even if he wasn't right, it was starting to feel like I didn't have a choice. How could I deny coach this request?

"Okay, Coach," I said, finally giving in to the inevitable. "I'll give Josh a call."

"Good," he said.

And then his eyes became sleepy. It was as if he could finally rest after getting me to commit.

But I didn't feel like I was committing to the job just yet. I needed to talk to Josh and have a few conversations first. One talk wasn't going to do it. This was big. I didn't know the first thing about being a head coach on the high school level, let alone coaching a team with the profile of Dunbar. I wasn't even old enough to legally buy a six-pack of beer.

"I hope you're right about this, Coach."

"I will be," he said. "You'll see."

I wasn't so sure, but that look in his eyes from a minute before stuck with me.

"I'm gonna go get something to drink from the cafeteria," I said. "You need anything?"

"Nah," he said before chuckling. "I'd love a cigar, but they'd have my head."

Cigars were what Coach Wilson loved best after a game, whether we won or lost.

"Okay, I'll be right back," I said.

I left his room and walked down the hallway to the elevator. It was then that I realized what I had just done and it scared the shit out of me. Here I was at twenty years old, just a year out of jail, with minimal—funny to even call it that—head coaching experience, and I had all but agreed to be the head coach at one of the most well-known basketball programs on the east coast. I thought of what the warden told me on the morning of my first day in jail and it couldn't have been truer. He said, "Life is a journey and it's winding and unpredictable. This is just a stop on that unpredictable road. When you get out of here, your job is to make sure that you never find yourself back in here because that would be predictable. You have to keep the mystery in your life."

The elevator arrived and it was just in time—because standing there waiting for it was making me question myself. Just in the few seconds it took for the elevator to rise up and meet me I nearly balked at what would be the most important decision in my life.

THREE

It was the middle of summer, so there wasn't much going on in the world of local high school sports. Football was still a couple of months from starting, meaning that basketball was an even more distant thought. But Dunbar's varsity basketball team didn't have a coach. Well, technically they still did, but he was in the hospital getting aggressive chemotherapy for a cancer that was just as aggressive. When they named a new head coach, the news would definitely make the *Times* and *Post*.

The day after promising Coach Wilson I would do so, I called Josh Allen early in the morning.

I couldn't sleep the night before. I was thinking about the opportunity—and the troubles—that it would bring.

Josh expected my call.

"Julius," he said. "How are you? Do you have good news for me?"

"You're on board with it too?"

"Yes. I think it's a great idea," he said, his voice booming like in his days as the starting quarterback at Dunbar. "This will work."

"How come I'm the only one who thinks that it won't?" I asked.

———

I arrived at Dunbar High School a little earlier than eleven o'clock. I could only pace around my tiny, one-bedroom apartment for so long. The woman working the front desk of the main office said that Josh was on a phone call until eleven. With every-one else on summer vacation, she was the only one there. I asked if I could go inside the gym to wait. She smiled and said "Of course."

I *had* been back to Dunbar to see Coach Wilson since getting out of jail. Being in the school wasn't a big deal to me. My reason for being there, on the other hand, felt anything but normal. It felt big, too big. I was at my old school walking through the main lobby and down the hall to the gym to takeover for Coach Wilson. I could feel his presence in the halls, and it didn't help matters that pictures of him and his teams hung on the walls and in the glass trophy case outside the gym. He built the basketball program with his own hands, and for some reason he chose to pass the torch to me.

I leaned in close to the glass case to find the team picture from my junior year. I found it. Coach Wilson was there in his three-piece suit with hair as dark as a summer night in southeast D.C., and there I was in the front row kneeling with the other guards. As usual, I had a frown on my face. That picture was taken one week before my life changed.

It was one week before John died, one week before I *really* had something to frown about.

I pushed open the double doors to the gym and walked inside. It was dark, and the black and red paint on the court signaling the school colors made the gym seem even darker. "Home of the Crimson Tide" was printed along both sidelines and on the far wall opposite the double doors. I walked to midcourt and stood on the school logo, which was a silly-looking wave with angry eyes and gritted teeth that was supposed to be a "crimson tide."

I continued over to the home team's bench. Chairs were lined up, fifteen or so, as if there was a game that night. I sat down in the chair that Coach Wilson sat in for twenty years. I looked up to the rafters and saw the five city championship banners among the countless other section titles.

I thought of Coach Wilson. He was dying and that would be bad for basketball in D.C. It would be bad for the youth of D.C. It would be a tragedy for me.

I checked my watch and it was five minutes to

eleven. I got up from Coach Wilson's chair and looked out to the court. I couldn't see myself out there playing anymore. That part of me was dead. I looked down and saw my feet in brown dress shoes standing outside the lines of the court. That was the first time I could see it. I could see myself as the coach of Dunbar. I could only see myself on the sidelines, though. I didn't exist inside those lines anymore.

———

"Hey, Josh," I said as I shook his hand inside his office. His hands were strong and his body was fit, just like during his playing days. Josh was about four years older than me. He was a two-star athlete at Dunbar, starting at quarterback in fall and coming off the bench as a backup guard for Coach Wilson in the spring. He was a D.C. legend with his pick of any college in either sport.

"Have a seat," he said with wide eyes and an equally wide smile.

"I'm going to ask you this one more time," I said. "Are you sure about this?"

"Yes."

He sat down at his desk and I did the same across from him.

"Because I was out there on the court while you were on the phone," I said, "and I felt *it*. I felt that I could do the job."

"We know you can," he said. "Coach Wilson and I."

"I've been going into see him almost every day," I said. "It doesn't look too good."

"I know it," he said. "I talked to the doctor yesterday while he was sleeping, and he doesn't know how much longer it'll be. The cancer is really aggressive."

I didn't say anything to that. I just let it settle into the air and then disappear.

"Which is why we need to hurry up and lock you in," he said, snapping us both out of our sadness. "As much time as he has left, is as much time that you'll have to pick his brain."

"I don't want to think about him going," I said.

"He's gonna go soon," he said. "We are all gonna have to face that truth."

"So when he got sick, he brought this idea to you? About having me take over for him?"

Josh nodded his head calmly. I remembered seeing him walk through the halls when I was a skinny, little freshman. He always looked calm to me in the halls, out on the field, and on the court.

"Coach Wilson did the same thing with me," he said. "After I tore up my knee during senior year of college, the NFL was out. I had a degree, but I really didn't have a plan. Coach got me a job as an assistant coach on the JV basketball team, plus a P.E. teacher position to, you know, kind of pay the bills. After one year, I was an assistant on his staff and one year after that, Reynolds was retiring and the athletic director position was open."

All of this happened while I was in jail.

"Coach Wilson put me up for it," he said. "He had to convince me that I could do the job. I had no idea what an athletic director did. But he knew. He knew I could do the job way before I knew it."

I couldn't say anything. All I could do was think about the look on Coach's face.

"He feels the same way about you," he said. "And so do I."

"Coach Wilson gave me this look yesterday," I said, "while I was at the hospital. It's probably bullshit, but that look was the thing that did it. Do you know what I'm talking about?"

"I do," he said. "Same thing happened with me."

There was silence again and Josh broke it by slapping a palm on his desk.

"First we need to talk about your pay," he said.

After Coach Wilson first offered the job, all my focus went to whether or not I could actually do the job. I didn't even think about the fact that they were going pay me. I could barely get by during that first year out of jail. I worked at an after-school center for at-risk youth every weekday from three to eight. I also picked up any odd job I could find to make a little extra. Any job I did had to be cleared with my parole officer first.

"Because you're just starting out, your salary will be thirty-five thousand dollars, plus medical and dental coverage. We'll talk 401K and pension when we do your contract." Josh said.

He could've said any number and I would've accepted. I couldn't help but smile when he mentioned that medical insurance and retirement were a part of the package. Where I was from—where I had been—those things didn't exist. They were for other people, not me.

"Also, once you get settled, you'll have to start working towards getting certified to teach in the classroom," he said. "Our coaches teach at least one class per semester. It's a way to connect with the school and not just the athletic department. You'll be enrolled in classes and you need to get that all taken care of on your time. Got me?"

"Absolutely. I have a bunch of the credits already," I said. "Coach helped me get my GED along with my associate's in education when I was inside."

"Bring in your credentials and I'll check with the administrators," he said. "We'll see what credits you still need, if any."

"Listen, Josh," I said. "I think before we go any further, we need to talk about, you know . . . "

"What?"

"How the public is going to react to the fact that the new head coach of Dunbar's basketball team was in jail just a year ago."

"I'm sure Coach Wilson talked to you about that," he said. "This could be something really big. You turned yourself around and it wasn't through sports. It could mean a lot to the kids to hear that kind of story. If we do it right."

"Do you guys think I can get the job done as a coach? Or is this more to help inspire kids in D.C.?"

He sighed. "I think it's both," he said. "The coaching part is where you'll have your biggest adjustment. You're going to be filling some pretty big shoes."

That didn't make me feel good and it almost took me back to the place where I didn't want the job, the place that made sense.

"But you've already gotten through the hard part," he insisted.

"Life is still hard for me day to day," I said.

"It is for everybody," he said as he got up from his chair and walked around to my side of the desk.

I stood up too.

"Let's have lunch and continue this."

We walked out of his office and back through the gym without saying a word. I walked behind him down the sideline, looking down at my shoes again. I made sure to stay outside the lines.

When we got into the main hallway, we walked side by side.

"The other thing," I said. "The *most important thing*. How are you going to sell hiring someone that isn't even twenty-one years old yet to such an important job?"

He looked at me sideways. "You'll be twenty-one by the time the season starts, right?"

"Yeah."

"Good. It'll be fine," he said. "We need some fresh blood here. And I mean that with the utmost respect for Coach Wilson. The community is going to get behind you, even if it takes some time."

"The coach of the football team is young too, right?" I asked.

"Yup, twenty-three years old," he said. "My first hire. Went one and ten his first year. Last season he took them all the way to the city championship and lost by three."

His face swelled with pride.

"Fresh blood, Julius," he said again. "Fresh blood would do this whole damn city good."

We walked out of the school and got into Josh's fresh-looking Jeep Cherokee. The outside of the car was red and the interior was black. He was Dunbar through and through.

FOUR

It was a nice summer day in D.C. The temperature wasn't in the nineties as it usually was during that time of year and there were periods of cloud cover overhead. Josh asked if I wanted to go to Old Ebbitt Grill for lunch. I had never been before, but I knew of it. Anybody who lived in D.C. knew about that place. It stood right next to The White House and opened in the mid-eighteen hundreds.

"Yeah," I said. "That sounds fine."

As we passed through the circle to stay on Massachusetts Avenue, I thought about my older brother John. When he started selling drugs and making money, he began going out to fancy restaurants around the city. He would get the newspaper and see where the hot spots were—not only the new ones, but the classics too, like Old Ebbitt. I remembered he told me about it after he ate there for the first time. He talked about the oysters and the Reuben sandwich. I had never eaten either of those things before. I didn't even know what they were. But I looked up to him so much that I wanted to eat there just like him. About a month before he was shot and killed, John promised that he would take me to Old Ebbitt Grill.

He never got the chance.

———

"Try the oysters," Josh said while looking through the menu.

The restaurant was dark and seemed crowded for that time of day. A lot of government types were there dressed in suits and drinking beer from glasses.

Josh ordered a half-dozen oysters for us to share

along with a couple of Reuben sandwiches. He ordered a beer while I took a Coke.

"You're gonna have to make a decision on what kind of staff you want," he said, taking a sip of his beer. "Coach Wilson's assistants are all older, experienced. You can keep them or hire a young set of assistants."

The waiter came back and set a tray of oysters down between us.

Josh took one in his hand. "You just squirt a little lemon on it and knock it back."

He tipped his head back and dropped the oyster down his throat. "Delicious," he said before taking another sip from his beer.

"You don't chew it?"

He chuckled at that. "Nah," he said. "You don't chew it."

I tried my first oyster and it *was* delicious.

"Coach Wilson's assistants won't wanna coach under me," I said, feeling bold from my first oyster. "I'm sure about that."

"Don't be so sure. We talked to a couple of them and they said they'd be on board," he said. "But you're right. There's a risk that they'll resent you or even undermine you."

Josh took another oyster and I did the same. After he finished it, he looked over to bar like he recognized someone.

"See that old black guy over there?" he asked.

I looked over to the bar and saw the man.

"That's Butch Teague," he said. "He is the reason I took you to lunch here. Was hoping we'd bump into him."

The name seemed familiar, but distant at the same time. I shook my head.

"You'll get to know him," he said. "He's the oldest high school sportswriter in this town. Been doing it for twenty-five years. I remember when I got this job. Coach Wilson introduced me to Butch the very first day. He said that it was important to have a good relationship with him."

"Butch!" Josh called out. "Butch!"

Butch turned around slowly with a glass of beer in hand.

Josh waved him over. Butch smiled, got off his stool, and walked over to us.

"Take a seat here, Butch," Josh said as they shook hands.

"Josh, you still look like you could play," he said with a smile. "You stalking me? You know I eat here every Tuesday."

"Let's just say I was hoping to bump into you," Josh said with an energetic smile of his own.

Butch took a seat and nodded to me.

"I want you to be the first to meet the new head coach of Dunbar's varsity basketball team," Josh said, gesturing to me. "Julius Crawford."

Butch looked at me and started to laugh. "Stop fucking with me, Josh," Butch said, jabbing a thumb in my direction. "How old is this kid?"

"He's turning twenty-one in—" Josh hesitated then looked over to me. "When is it again?"

"A month," I said.

Josh turned back to Butch. "A month."

Butch laughed again. And this time Josh joined in. It didn't feel great that these two men were sitting there laughing at my expense, and right in my face, no less. But I got it. It was crazy. The whole idea was nuts.

They finally stopped laughing and Butch took a big sip from his beer.

"Come on Josh, give it to me straight," he said. "Who are you guys looking at? I hear you guys sent word to Nixon over at Roosevelt that the job was his if he wanted it."

Josh took a sip from his beer and shook his head methodically. "Not true. This is our guy."

"Coach Wilson know about this?" Butch asked.

"This was his idea," Josh said. "Actually, both of ours."

Butch looked at me again. He didn't laugh this time. He just looked me over.

"This doesn't make a whole hell of a lot of sense,

Josh," he said. "I know that *you* are young and have been pretty successful over there, but . . . "

"Once you get to know him," Josh said, "you'll see."

Butch didn't say anything to that.

"We want you to break the story, Butch," Josh said. "The high school sports cycle is dead right now, right? But the area is waiting on this decision. Coach Wilson getting sick is big news. We're going back to the office right now to sign the contract, start putting together the staff, and all that fun stuff, but I want you to break it. This is gonna be big news. And when's he's successful, it's going to be even bigger."

He looked over at me, "You sure you wanna do this, kid?"

Josh cut in before I could answer. "This is our guy," Josh said as he finished his beer.

"If this is true," Butch said, "and if you're not just drunk, I'll break it."

"Good," Josh said.

"But the public will want more than that," Butch said. "I'll have to write a profile on him. See why on God's green earth you people decided to give one of the most important high school basketball head coaching jobs in the country to a kid."

"A profile would be good," Josh said with another smile. "I was thinking the same thing."

Butch handed me a card with his name and phone number on it. The heading on the card read: *The Washington Times*, Lead Beat Writer - Local High School Sports.

"After you get settled, give a me a call and we'll talk," Butch said.

"Okay," I said.

Butch got up from the table, looked me over one more time, and shook his head.

"This is either gonna be a big success," Butch said, "or you are gonna be looking for a job as a P.E. teacher, Josh."

They shook hands again and Butch left the table. He walked past the bar and out of the restaurant.

"This is good, Julius," Josh said. "It'll get your name out there before you even coach a game."

"This is a risk, Josh," I said. "What if he writes an article about how I am not qualified? What if all he wants to talk about is my days in prison?"

Josh didn't say anything to that right away. We both didn't touch our food. Nerves killed my appetite. We both just looked around at the lack of movement in the restaurant. There wasn't a lot of energy. Most of the customers were older, but Josh and I were different. We had youth on our side. Still, I could tell that the realness of the situation had sunk in for Josh, too. It was no longer just my ass on the line.

"You could lose *your* job," I said.

"You don't think *I* know that?" he asked.

He signaled to the waiter and asked him to bring the bill.

"Let's get back to the office and wrap this up," he said as he took out his credit card from his wallet. "We have some important shit to do."

"Like picking the staff," I said.

"That and meeting *your* players," he said. "They deserve to know before the public does."

Through all that was going on I forget to think about the players.

"Yeah," I said dimly. "The players."

"*Your* players."

FIVE

It was midnight by the time we finished up my contract and decided whom to keep on the coaching staff. There was obviously no time left in the day to meet any of the players, and that was good because I had no energy to do so.

Josh would introduce me to the three best and most experienced players on the team at three o'clock the next afternoon. He gave me a ride home that night. When he saw where I lived, he told me to start looking for a new apartment. He also told me to look for a car.

I asked him if he knew someone that could help me with that and he said he did. Before dropping me off, he reminded me again to call Butch in the morning.

I got out of his car and the air was still warm, but not unpleasant. There were a few guys hanging out in front of my building. I walked by them and got a couple of hard stares. Even though they knew me from the building, they didn't really *know* me. I didn't hang with them.

It was steamy inside my apartment. I opened all the windows and grabbed a Coke from the fridge. I sat at the window in my tiny living room. I could see the darkened shadow of Capitol Hill in the distance. I thought of Coach Wilson sitting in his hospital bed, smiling after Josh called him with the news. I owed him so much and it made me sad that he wasn't going to get the chance to see me coach.

I was tired—from the day, from life. I needed a good night's sleep before the news broke to the whole D.C. area. I was starting to feel . . . excited?

By nine o'clock the next morning, I was ready to take on the world. I had a quick breakfast before calling Butch. We agreed to meet at my apartment at noon.

Butch was right on time. I met him in front of my building, and the temperature was already in the high nineties. He wiped the sweat off his forehead as he glanced up at my building.

He laughed quietly.

"I'm hoping for a miracle and you have air conditioning up there," he said. "But I doubt it."

I didn't say anything. I just walked into the building and he followed me up the two flights of stairs to my apartment. I stopped at my front door and turned back to Butch. "It's not a terrible place to live," I said.

"Take it easy," he said. "It's just a joke."

"I lived in way worse places growing up," I said.

I opened the door to my apartment and we went inside.

"Want something to drink?" I asked.

"Anything that's cold."

I pulled a Coke out of the fridge and handed it to him with a glass. He took a seat on the couch and whipped out his pen and notepad. I was expecting him to record our conversations with a tape recorder or maybe his phone. I thought that people in jail were the only ones who still used pens and paper.

He nodded and opened his Coke. He took a big sip followed by a smaller one.

I took a seat on a chair across from the couch.

"How does this work?" I asked.

"How does what work?"

"This," I said. "I don't even know what *this* is."

"You talked to Coach Wilson today?"

"Last night."

"And how was he?"

"You know," I said. "Not good. But he's fighting."

"Coach Wilson is a good man," he said.

I nodded.

"The way this works is you tell me a bunch

of shit about yourself, your life, your past, your family," he said. "And how you feel about getting this job."

He paused to take another sip of soda and wipe some more sweat from his brow.

"And then I do what I do," he said.

I sighed.

"You don't seem too thrilled about this," he said.

"I just don't think my life story is anything that needs to be written about," I said.

Butch got up off the couch. "Well, that's good to know," he said as he started walking toward the door. "My work here is done."

"Wait!" I said, standing up from the chair. "Where are you going?"

"I'm going to the bar," he said after turning around. "It's way too hot in here and if you don't want to do it, we won't do it. You're doing me no favors here."

"Alright, I get it," I said. "Just tell me what to do."

"You supply me with what I need and I'll do the rest," he said. "We work together. I ain't trying to hurt you—I'm looking for a story. What kind of story you give me is gonna be up to you. If you don't feed me a story and let me write it, somebody else is gonna write your story for me. And that somebody won't know shit about you. You feel me?"

"Okay," I said. "I feel you."

He sat back down on the couch, and I did the same on the chair.

"Let's talk about what led you to jail," he said. "That's a start, and that's the part people are gonna be asking questions about from day one."

I took a deep breath. "Well that's not such an easy story," I said. "It's not like I woke up one morning at seventeen years old and found myself in jail."

"Ok," he said. "Start at the beginning."

He crossed his legs and leaned back on the couch.

"The beginning," I said. "Okay."

He took his pen and jabbed it against a fresh page in the notepad.

"Aren't you going to record this or something?" I asked.

"Nah," he said with a smile and a tip of his pen, "I'm old school."

———

"Yo Ju," he said. "Ju, where you at?"

I opened my eyes and slowly the sleep fell from them. The heat was all around me. It seemed like there were only a few things you could count on in D.C. and the weather was one of them. Hot in the summer; cold in the winter. Niggas killing each other in the neighborhood—that was another one.

I went to the window to see which skinny, little

nigga was down there calling up to me. I looked down and saw that it was Aaron, one of my closest boys.

"What up?" I called down to him.

"Why you in the house so early?" he asked.

"It's too hot," I said. "It's too hot to be out on the corner. It's too hot to drink. It's too hot to fuck. So I just said, 'fuck it,' I'm gonna go to sleep."

"It's never too hot to fuck," he said as he wiped some sweat from under his Wizards hat.

"Where you staying at tonight?"

"Ah," he said, "I'm thinking 'bout going to Chantel's house. But I'm not ready to go in yet. Your brothers are over there at Ray's crib. They 'bout to break out. Call a bunch of hos over."

I looked up at the city and the sky was black.

"John and Myron are over there?" I asked.

"Yeah."

"They ask about me?"

"Nah, nigga," he said before spitting. "Are you gonna come or is you gonna stay in bed like a bitch?"

He grinned.

"Gimme ten minutes," I said before grabbing a pair of jeans and a white T off of the floor.

I walked out of my room and through the hallway into the living room. My mom was asleep on the couch and the TV was turned on with the volume halfway up. All the lights were on, too. I knew not to touch it or else she would wake up. I only turned the lights off. The lights didn't matter.

I met Aaron downstairs and we shook. He was tough, and also crazy. He could fight and wasn't afraid to pull a gun on someone who was a better fighter.

"Shit's crazy around the way," he said.

"Another one?"

"Another two," he said. "They found two of Pooh's boys dead in the street a couple of hours ago. One yesterday down there off Eastern, and three earlier in the week."

"Niggas is wildin'," I said as we started down the sidewalk towards Ray's.

"That's why I got this," he said as he raised his

shirt and exposed his waistband. I could see the grip of his Glock nine. "What about you?"

I waved my hand at the air.

"Yeah, you don't need one," he said. "No one's gonna fuck with you 'cause of your brothers. But me? I'm a free agent. Ain't no angels sittin' on my shoulders."

"You never shut the fuck up, you know that?"

"You gonna play at Dunbar this season?" he asked, changing the subject. "I heard your brothers talking about how they want you to stop slinging so you can focus on basketball."

"Man, I don't know."

I didn't like people talking about my life without me there to talk for myself, even my own brothers. They made their own choices. And I wanted to do the same. I didn't buy in to that big-brother-watching-out-for-the-little-brother shit.

We got to Ray's house. I could hear the bass thumping from inside along with the giggles and screams of the ladies. You couldn't just walk up and get into Ray's parties. You had to be someone in the neighborhood.

I knocked on the door.

"You gotta knock harder than that!" Aaron said. "They in there breakin' out."

He pounded on the door three times.

We could hear the music being turned down, then heavy footsteps coming towards the door. They had to be Ray's.

The door opened slowly and Ray poked his big head out. His eyes were wide open. You couldn't tell that he was drunk and high off his ass.

His eyes relaxed when he saw us.

"What are you two little niggas doing here knocking like you the damn police?" he asked.

"You paranoid," Aaron said as he stepped through the doorway.

"Hey John!" Ray called back into his apartment. "Your little big-head brother is here with his monkey-ass friend."

The music was turned back up to full volume and the party resumed. There were a whole bunch of players from the neighborhood and girls from around the way too. Every guy there seemed to have his own girl. Some of them had two.

On the way to the back of the house where my brothers were, we stopped in the kitchen. Aaron grabbed a forty from the fridge and held a second one out for me. I waved it off.

"Why you ain't drinkin'?" he asked before cracking the seal and taking a big sip.

"I just got here, nigga," I said. "Why you all over me?"

"Alright, alright," he said.

Even though the music was loud, I could hear my brothers in the back of the house—the part of the house reserved for only the most important players at Ray's parties. Their low voices registered instantly, waking up all kinds of memories inside of me. I walked on through the kitchen and through the curtain that separated it from the back room. Aaron followed behind.

My brothers were sitting at a table that was set up in the corner of the room. There were stacks of money all around them neatly banded and organized by denomination. There was also a trash bag on the floor near the table. I knew what was inside it. Those were the "dirty" bills, the ones that needed to be counted, organized and banded. Ray's back room wasn't a VIP room or anything like you'd see in a club. It was the counting room is all.

John looked up from the bills and saw me standing in the doorway. He nodded and then there was this strange look on his face. I couldn't tell if he was upset or not. Myron had his back to me and was busy with his count.

I walked over and put a hand on Myron's shoulder.

He jumped with a spasm, turned around, and smiled when he saw me.

"You lucky it's you," he said. "Real lucky."

"What are you doing here?" John asked.

"I don't know," I said. "You know, I couldn't sleep and I heard you guys were here."

"We're always here," he said. "You ain't answer my question."

"I wanted to see if you needed any help countin'," I said.

John looked to Myron and they both smiled.

"How's mama?" John asked.

"She's fine," I said.

"That motherfucker Anthony been around?" John asked.

"A little," I said. "Not as much a before."

"I'ma have to smoke that fool if he keep hangin' around you and mama," John said. "Or at least get someone to do it for me."

"It's all good," I said.

"How are you?" John asked.

"I'm good, you know," I said. "Tryin' to grind."

"Things are crazy out there right now," John said. "It's better if your ass is in school."

I didn't say anything to that.

"You're going to Dunbar this year, right?" he added. "You're playing ball aren't you?"

I still didn't say anything.

"Getting up with Coach Wilson'll do some good for you," he said.

"I don't know," I said. "Everybody says that he be hard on niggas."

"That's what you need," John said. "Li'l punk."

John's eyes looked past me to the door. I turned and saw Ray walking someone in. I thought I recognized the kid. He looked like one of Pooh's boys from around the way.

"We'll finish this later, Ju," John said.

I could see the seriousness in his face. His eyes got that cold look in them; the look said it was time to put in work.

"You need to get on out of here," he said, standing up from the table. "Get Aaron and roll on out. I'll catch you tomorrow at the house."

Myron stood up from the table as well.

I turned around and looked at the boy standing there with Ray behind him. He was shook. Definitely looked like he wasn't there to break out. Definitely looked like he was forced to be there. I started to walk out of the room and grabbed Aaron by the arm. When I walked by the boy, I smelled piss and Ray, standing there behind him, smelled it too.

John called out to me before we got to the door: "Julius!"

I turned around.

"I love you," he said.

I knew John loved me—he always looked out for me and tried to keep me on the straight path as much as he could. But I never heard him say it, especially not in public like that.

I turned and we left the party.

When we got outside, a siren from a few blocks away screamed through the air. Aaron threw his empty bottle against the street, shattering it.

"Why we gotta leave?" he asked in a loud voice. I could hear the beer in his voice.

"We just had to."

"That was one of Pooh's boys," he said.

I nodded.

"What you think—"

I stared at Aaron and he swallowed the rest of his words.

The sound of the siren faded, and then was gone. The only sounds left were bits of broken glass crunching beneath our shoes.

"Where you going?" Aaron asked. "To the crib?"

"Yeah," I said.

He didn't say anything. He just put his hands in his pockets.

"What about you?" I asked.

"I think I'm gonna go see what's up with Chantel," he said.

"Watch yourself, hear?" I said. "Shit is hot right now."

"Yeah," he said. "I'll get at you tomorrow."

We shook hands and Aaron continued down the street, walking in and out of the light from the street lamps until he was consumed by the darkness.

———

"How old were you then?" Butch asked. "The night of that party."

"I had just turned fifteen," I said. "About to start at Dunbar."

"And did you have any contact with Coach

Wilson up to that point? Were you good enough to make varsity as a freshman?"

"I knew Coach Wilson. We met a few times at basketball camps, AAU tournaments," I said. "I was a good player, known around town, but not a superstar. Once I committed to going to school, Coach Wilson wanted me to play. I played JV during freshman year and then half of sophomore year before moving up."

Butch scribbled in his notepad.

"I remember during the summers, my older brother John would send me to all the basketball camps around the city. Even though I loved playing, I would have rather spent time with him. But he would tell me that I had to go. He paid good money for all of them. I went to two or three camps a summer starting in the sixth grade."

"That's where I want to go next," Butch said. "I want to know more about John."

The heat in the room rested in the pit of my

stomach and then shot all the way up to my head. Dizzy, I checked my watch and it was one-thirty. Plenty of time before I had to be at Dunbar, but I was done talking for the day.

"We have to stop here, Butch."

"What?" he asked, looking down at his watch. "I thought you said we had until two, two-fifteen?"

"I have to stop now," I said. "I have to get up to school. Meet my players."

That sounded strange coming out of my mouth.

Butch gave me an uncertain look. I'm sure with all of his experience he knew that talking about my past would bring up some pain, and he would have been right if he thought that. Thoughts of John always brought pain with them, no matter how much time had passed.

"Okay, Julius," Butch said calmly. "We'll pick this up . . . I guess . . . "

"Tomorrow," I said.

"Tomorrow."

He got up from the couch and gathered his

things. I walked him to the door and he turned around to face me before opening the door.

"What happened to Aaron?" he asked. "It's not important for your story. I'm just curious. It seemed like trouble was close to finding him."

"Two days after that party at Ray's, Aaron was found on a corner near Minnesota Avenue and Good Hope," I said. "Two shots in the back of his head."

SIX

I called Josh for a ride to school and he picked me up on his way. He asked me about my first meeting with Butch and I said it went fine. He didn't press for more details. Meeting with Butch made it feel real. The pressure was all around me and I hadn't even held one practice yet, let alone a game. I was already tired of being under the microscope.

When we got to school and walked into the gym, there were three players standing around the key shooting standstill jumpers. Two of them were guards and the other one was a power forward.

They weren't wearing basketball gear. They wore jeans and large white T-shirts instead.

Josh and I approached and their eyes caught mine.

"Julius, here are three of your most important players," Josh said. "This is Tremaine."

Tremaine was one of the guards. We shook hands.

"What's up, Coach?" he said.

"Tremaine."

"This is Dante," Josh said.

Dante was the other guard. He nodded and we shook.

"And this is Patrick," Josh said.

Patrick was the power forward.

"Nice to meet you, Coach," he said before shaking my hand.

"Patrick," I said.

Josh clapped his hands once. "Okay, I'm gonna leave you guys to it. Take as much time as you need. Dante, come see me after you're done with Coach."

Josh left the gym. The heavy clicks of his dress shoes on the hardwood echoed and the sound filled the entire gym. I waited until he was gone before saying anything to the players.

"What did you three think when you heard I was taking the job?" I asked. "Be honest."

The three of them looked at each other first. No one wanted to be the first to speak.

"Do you guys know about me?" I asked. "About my past?"

Tremaine shifted and I nodded to him.

"I do," he said. "My brother went to school with you. He said you went to jail."

"Who is your brother?" I asked.

"Tywon. Used to go by 'Ty.'"

That name, "Ty," brought a smile to my face. The two of us used to go at it one-on-one every day before practice.

"I knew your brother well," I said. "How is he?"

"He good," Tremaine said.

"I did go to jail," I said. "And if you guys want to know anything about it, just ask."

They didn't say anything.

"Things are going to be a lot different without Coach Wilson," I said. "We're all going to have to adjust, and we need to help each other."

Dante rolled his eyes and shook his head.

"Dante," I said. "Question?"

He looked away from me for a moment and then set his eyes right at mine.

"Nah," he said. "No question."

"Okay," I said.

Patrick was the only one of the three who looked like he wanted to be there. His lanky frame was loose and his face held a gentle smile.

"What about you, big man?" I asked.

His smile became even wider. Tremaine and Dante didn't smile at all. Five minutes with them told me a lot about their personalities.

"I'm just excited is all," Patrick said before looking to his two teammates. "I'm excited about playing for you, Coach."

It was strange being called "Coach," but it was something I could get used to.

"You guys are my leaders," I said. "Whatever plans I have for the team, you guys will know about them first. I want you guys to lead during games, on the practice floor, and off the floor as well."

Dante rolled his eyes again.

"Looks like there's something wrong with your eyes," I said.

"What?" Dante said with his eyes narrowing.

"Your eyes," I said. "They're not working right."

The gym was tense. I didn't plan on starting out this way, it just happened. Dante was testing me in front of Tremaine and Patrick. Just like out on the streets, if you back down just once there's no getting it back.

"How about this?" I asked. "Me and Patrick versus you and Tremaine?"

Dante turned to Tremaine and laughed.

"Is he serious?" he asked.

"You up?" I asked.

Dante thought about it for a moment before taking his white T-shirt off. He tightened the belt around his jeans, pulled his undershirt off, and threw it off to the side.

"Game is to eleven by ones," I said.

I picked one of the balls off the floor and fired it to Dante. He caught it and stared straight back at me. Patrick took Tremaine and I took Dante.

"Shoot for ball?" he asked.

"You guys take it," I said.

I could tell by his body language that Dante was uneasy, but I didn't care. Josh said that he was one of my best players and I didn't care about that either. I needed to see it for myself.

We checked the ball and Dante passed it to Tremaine. He dribbled around the key for a while and Patrick stayed right with him. He could move his feet for a big man. That combined with his long arms was the makings of a defensive stopper.

Tremaine passed the ball to Dante and he came right at me, leaving the confused look behind. I stayed on his right hand to see if he could go left, and when he hesitated to cross the ball over, I knew that he had a weakness. I ripped the ball from his right hand and we took possession.

I motioned for Patrick to go into the post, because the height and wingspan difference between him and Tremaine was ridiculous. I floated a pass to him on the right block and he showed me that he had decent offensive game to go along with his defense. He took a drop step when he felt Tremaine leaning too hard, and put the ball in off the glass for the first point.

"Nice footwork," I said, slapping high-five with Patrick.

"This shit ain't fair," Tremaine whined. "I'm not gonna be guarding someone as tall as him in a game."

"Stop crying," I said. "What happens if you get switched on a big man during a game? It happens all the time."

Tremaine didn't say anything.

We scored three more points before they got the ball back, all of them on post-ups from Patrick.

Tremaine tried to stop him even though he was at a severe height disadvantage and I liked that. What I didn't like, though, was that Dante didn't go down to help Tremaine on defense or even volunteer to switch onto Patrick.

We were up four to nothing before they scored their first points. Dante got me on my heels with a hesitation dribble and when he had enough space, he stepped back for a sweet jumper behind the three-point line. Too bad we were only playing by ones.

"Nice shot," I said.

He didn't reply.

It was four to three when Patrick blocked Dante's drive to the hoop. I grabbed the ball out of the air and took it out to the three-point line to clear it. I called for Patrick to come out and screen Dante. When he did, Dante made no effort to get through the screen and I went in for the easy layup.

Five to three, our way.

"Damn, nigga!" Tremaine said to Dante. "Ain't you gonna fight through the screen?"

"You're supposed to back me up," Dante fired back. "Not just let that motherfucker walk right in for the layup!"

I got in between them.

"Watch your mouth, Dante," I said, putting a hand up to his chest. "Don't talk to your teammate like that."

He wiped my hand away.

"You don't tell me shit," he said. "You ain't no coach."

"Dante," I said. "Relax."

"Fuck you!" he said.

He grabbed the ball off the floor and threw it to the other end of the gym.

"Fuck this," he said before walking past me.

"Dante!" I said.

He ignored me.

"Dante!"

He stopped at the doors and looked back at me. There was hurt in his eyes. I could see it from all the way across the gym. I knew that look. He turned around and left the gym. The door slammed shut and the metallic echo settled into silence.

I looked to Tremaine and Patrick.

Tremaine stayed quiet. Patrick did too, but his eyes told me that he wanted to say something.

"Ok," I said. "You guys can go. I'll be tough throughout the summer. Good luck with AAU."

There were rules about contact with players over the summer. Technically, our little two-on-two game was against those rules. The only contact I was allowed to have with the players was off the court and for no more than thirty minutes at a time.

Tremaine walked past me without saying a word. Patrick stayed behind, waiting for Tremaine to exit the gym.

"Dante was really close to Coach Wilson," he said. "I mean, we all were."

"I know," I said. "Me too."

"But it goes deeper with Dante," he continued. "After Dante's mom passed, Coach Wilson let

Dante stay at his house until his aunt could take him in. It saved him from having to go to Social Services."

"How did his mother pass?"

"She died on the streets," he said. "They found her with a needle in her arm."

I didn't say anything to that.

"That's what I heard, anyway," he said.

"Okay, Patrick," I said. "Stay healthy this summer. I'm gonna need you ready to go by the time the season starts."

"Got ya, Coach," he said.

There was that word "coach" again. It still sounded strange.

Patrick started to leave the gym.

"Patrick!" I called out to him.

He turned around and looked at me.

"Thanks for being cool about this," I said. "I'm gonna need your help along with Tremaine and Dante's. The other guys will follow."

"I'll help as much as I can, Coach," he said

with another genuine smile. "Tremaine will come around eventually. Dante, I don't know."

———

"How'd it go?" Josh asked as I sat down in front of him at his desk.

"It went," I said.

"It's just the first day," he said.

"Is it too late to back out of this?" I asked, half-joking. "I don't even have a car or a decent place to live . . . I mean, how am I gonna—"

"Calm down," Josh said, leaning back in his chair so that it squealed under the weight of his body. "Dominique in the main office, she's gonna find an apartment for you. And tomorrow, I'm gonna take you to look at a cheap used car to get you to and from school."

I didn't have a response. I just sighed.

"Look, you're gonna make it," he said.

I still had nothing to say.

"How was Dante?"

I shook my head. "He's a hard kid," I said. "Angry."

"Yeah, he is," Josh said. "That right there will be your biggest challenge."

"I don't think I started out on the right foot with him."

"Dante is your best player. Tremaine and Patrick are good, really good. But they don't come anywhere close to Dante's athletic ability or his basketball IQ."

"He stormed out of the gym just now. I think I might've made a mistake back there," I said. "Came on too strong. Too fast."

"Well, Dante can play. He's got a big mouth. But you get him out there on that court with some direction and he can lead the team."

"And let me guess," I said. "Coach Wilson gave him direction."

Josh smiled.

"He's really tight with Coach Wilson," he said.

"Yeah, Patrick told me about his mother."

"When Coach Wilson got sick," he said, "Dante took it hard. He went to go visit him once and he couldn't go back again because Coach is in such bad shape."

"I don't know if I can get through to him," I said. "He needs to get that anger up out of him."

I jabbed my thumb into the air behind me towards the gym.

"Wanna go see Coach?" Josh asked.

"Yeah," I said.

"I heard you met with Butch earlier today."

"Yeah," my voice rose slightly, "and that's another thing—I'm not sure if putting myself out there like that is the right thing. It's personal. Folks around the way, and ones that aren't around the way, all of them, they'll judge me."

"You're right, some people will read it and judge you. But the rest of the people will read it and maybe they'll see things another way. We can count on Butch. He's an honest guy and he'll at least tell *your* story—not some bullshit version of it."

I thought about that for a second and nodded. I wanted to believe in what he was saying, but I still couldn't see it. The doubt was there and all I knew to do to get rid of it—other than quit—was to wake up the next day and try again.

"Let's roll out," he said. "Visiting hours at the hospital end soon. Coach Wilson asked me to come by with you."

SEVEN

"There he is!" Coach Wilson said before coughing violently.

His condition was worse than it was just a couple days before. His skin was a little more pale, and his head a little more bald.

"Hey Coach," I said with a smile that tried to disguise my concern.

"Come over here and give me a hug," he said.

I walked over to his bed and leaned down for a hug. All I could feel were bones. All the muscle and fat had disappeared underneath his skin.

"You made the right choice," he said.

"Josh keeps telling me the same thing," I said, sitting down in a chair next to his bed.

"Where is Josh?"

"He's on the phone."

"I'm really happy about this, son," he said.

I felt uncomfortable sitting there talking about basketball while he was in a hospital bed fighting for his life.

"How are you, Coach?" I asked.

"Oh you know, there's not a lot of time left for me," he said with a knowing smile. The calm in his voice and on his face helped me to relax a little.

"When I was up in that jail cell," I said, "wondering if this was gonna be it for me, you were the only one that reached out."

"No need to go back over it," he said. "Keep looking in front of you, Julius. It's all there for the taking."

Josh walked in and stopped at the door. His face turned serious when he saw Coach's condition.

"How you feeling, Coach?"

"We were just talking about you," Coach said.

"We finally convinced him," Josh said, patting me on the back. "It took a while, but we did it."

"Now I can die happy," Coach said before laughing and coughing again.

"You're gonna fight this," Josh said. "You're gonna be there in the stands to watch Julius coach his first game."

"The doc says I'll be gone way before then," Coach said.

"Doctors can be wrong," Josh said in a voice that started to shake.

"They'd have to be dead wrong for me to make it to that first game."

"Where's Rose?" I asked, changing the subject.

I hadn't seen Coach's wife since he'd first gotten sick. When I played for Coach, she was like a mother to me—more so than even my own mother. She used to cook for a few of the other guys on the team and me, and we'd sit down at the dinner table with her, Coach, and their son,

TJ. Those meals meant a lot to a kid like me who didn't know what it meant to be in a real family.

"She's downstairs at the cafeteria with TJ," Coach said. "They sit here all day and night just staring at me, crying. I tell them it does no good."

"How is TJ?" I asked.

TJ was around Josh's age and was a young assistant coach at Dunbar during the last season I played for Coach Wilson, the season I got in trouble.

"He's good," Coach said. "He's an assistant down at Coastal Carolina."

I smiled.

"He's really happy for you, too," Coach said.

"Hey Coach," Josh said. "Butch got up with Julius earlier today. He's gonna write a story about him in the *Post*."

Coach slowly looked away from Josh and centered his eyes on me. Everything about him was slow: his breathing, his eyes, his words. When I played for him, it was the opposite. Everything was about movement. He hated wasting anything, whether it was time, words, or energy. And for Coach Wilson, there was nothing worse than wasted movement out on the basketball court.

"Butch is a good man, Julius," Coach said. "If you give it to him fair, he'll write it fair."

"It's hard," I said. "But I'm gonna tell it to him how it really happened."

Coach nodded slowly. His eyelids started getting heavy.

"Did you meet any of the kids yet?" he asked, almost as a whisper.

"I met Tremaine, Dante, and Patrick," I said.

"Tremaine and Patrick will fall in," he said. "How was Dante?"

I glanced to Josh and he had a blank look on his face. I had to go at it alone.

"It wasn't the best first meeting," I said. "But it will get better."

Coach didn't buy it.

"I'll help you with Dante," he said. "He is a

special player. Off the floor is where you'll need my help."

"I guess some things never change," I said.

"I'll call him in the morning," he said.

"Coach, we're gonna head out," Josh said. "You need your rest."

Coach grabbed my forearm as I stood up from the chair.

"We need to talk strategy," he said. "You have any ideas yet about how you want to play?"

"Yeah, I have an idea," I said.

"Well spit it out!" Coach said with a short burst of energy.

I stood looking at Coach and then at Josh with what was most likely a nervous look on my face. I knew they were going to give me a hard time when I told them how I wanted my team to play.

"I want to run the triangle," I said.

Coach just stared at me for a second, and then he smiled. He looked to Josh and he too cracked a smile. Then they both started to laugh. Not just chuckles, but real laughs from deep down in the gut.

"The triangle?" Coach asked.

"I think it could work," I said.

Josh came and patted me on the shoulder.

"We need to go, Coach," he said, still laughing. "I think the job is starting to go his head."

"If you're serious," Coach said, "good luck. Because kids these days aren't going to buy into that offense without you really pushing them. Hell, I wouldn't have when I played high school ball."

"It's just a thought," I said, quickly second-guessing myself.

Coach smiled again, but this time it was weaker. He was running low on energy. Usually when talking about basketball, he could keep the conversation going for hours. A couple of weeks after I got out of jail, he invited me to his house for dinner and we stayed up until three in the morning talking hoops. Strategies, players, coaches—you name it, we talked about it. He wasn't sick then. At least I didn't know he was.

"Whatever offense you choose," Coach said, "you'll be successful. The triangle," he said with a smile. "Bold."

That was the last thing he said before closing his eyes and falling asleep. It was one thing to have others believe in me, but another to have *Coach* believe in me. I knew I could never live up to his record on the court; I would never win as many games as he did or match the city championship titles—he won five. Off the court was really where I wanted to follow in Coach Wilson's footsteps. Over the years, he had helped many kids get off the streets and into college. I had to somehow live up to that part of it too.

Josh and I walked out of Coach's room toward the elevator. We didn't say much about his condition because there wasn't much to say. As we waited, Josh's phone buzzed a few times and he looked down to read the messages. His face changed.

"Wow," he said.

He didn't look up from his phone until the elevator came and its door opened. It was empty. We stepped in and rested against the back wall. Josh put his phone in his pocket and pressed the button for the lobby. The door closed and we went down.

"It's a good thing that you are thinking about a ball-sharing offense like the triangle," he said.

I looked at him to see if he was joking and there was not even hint of a smile on his face.

"Why?" I asked.

"Because Dante is gone."

"Gone?" I asked. "He's dead?"

"Dead? What? No," he said. "He's transferring to Georgetown Prep."

The elevator stopped at the lobby.

"Your job just got a lot harder," Josh said as the door opened.

EIGHT

A month had passed since I talked to Butch that first time at my apartment. Things got busy when Dunbar officially hired me. Between hiring a coaching staff, meeting everyone at Dunbar, and changing apartments, there was no extra time to meet with him about the article in the *Post*.

Butch wasn't upset, though. He understood that I didn't have any free time and we agreed that the article would come out a few days before Dunbar's first regular season game, giving him around two months to write the article.

Coach Wilson was still alive. His condition was the same, with some good days and some bad. But when he heard the news of Dante transferring to Georgetown Prep, he had a rough time with it. Josh and I weren't sure he was going to make it through that.

Coach tried to get Dante to change his mind, but it was no use. Dante told Coach that he wasn't going to put his future in the hands of such a young coach, a coach with no experience. There was a rumor around town that Georgetown University had offered Dante a scholarship if he transferred to Georgetown Prep.

There were whispers about me, too. Well, more than whispers. The local media slammed the move to hire me, calling it a publicity stunt. Josh came to my defense, but he was also ridiculed.

Dunbar went out of its way to protect me in that first month after I was hired. I wasn't forced to do interviews with anyone other than Butch. I can't say that the criticism didn't hurt, because it did. All of the questions about my character from the media brought back the fears that I had at the very beginning—the idea that this was a mistake and that I was in way over my head. The first day of the school year, though, I sat in my office—Coach Wilson's old office—with a placard on my desk that read *Julius Crawford – Head Basketball Coach.*

———

When the school year started at Dunbar, I began taking night classes for my teaching credential. The only class I was able to teach during my first semester was P.E. I taught three periods throughout the day.

One day in late September, Butch agreed to meet me for an interview in my office.

"Julius," Butch said as he walked into the office.

I stood up from my desk and walked over to meet him. We shook hands. He looked around the office and I returned to my seat.

"You look a little funny in the big chair."

"I know," I said. "I'm still not used to it."

"You're taking a lot of hits out there," he said. "People sure love to talk shit, don't they?"

I shrugged and shook my head.

"Where'd we leave off last time?" Butch asked. "It was during the summer. You had just left a party where you saw your two brothers."

"Yeah," I said. "I remember."

———

I was just a sophomore, but good enough to be brought up to varsity toward the end of the season.

The first few practices up there were rough. I didn't think I was going to make it. Coach Wilson was hard on us.

You were going to do things his way or not do them at all.

He would ride me in practice. If I made a mistake once, he would just look at me and tell me how to correct it, but if I made the same mistake twice, he would be on me for the rest of practice. The other coaches told me it was because he saw something in me. I couldn't see it that way, though. It felt like an attack. Just like when you're out on the corner and someone looks at you the wrong way. It's war out there. To me, Coach Wilson's gym felt the same way.

Things at home were bad. Not any worse than usual, but still bad. Anthony was hanging out with my mom more and more. After a while, he was just there all the time doing nothing but getting high and watching TV. My mom didn't ask me what I thought about him moving in. She didn't care. She was right there with him, hitting the pipe, falling asleep on that fuckin' couch.

My brothers stopped coming around when Anthony moved in. I think it was because my mom begged them not to. They didn't think much of Anthony. Said he was a crack-fiend. If it wasn't for my mom, John and Myron would've killed Anthony. I was sure of it.

I remember one practice where Coach was all over

my ass, picking on me for every little thing. I had just had enough. I was so angry that I couldn't play. I just walked out of practice without telling anyone.

It was probably for the best, because I felt the anger inside of me and it was getting ready to come out. I could've easily taken it out on a teammate or maybe even Coach. When I left the gym, no one came after me. Not Coach, not any of my teammates, no one.

I changed clothes quick and left school. It really felt like it would be my last time there. I didn't belong in school, and even worse, I was starting to feel like I didn't belong on the court.

On my walk home from school, I saw John parked close to where my mom lived. He was easy to spot because of his brand new Mercedes SE convertible.

With one look at my face, he knew something was up. He grilled me about being home early from practice. I lied and said we got out early. Then he asked me if it was Anthony troubling me and if he and Myron needed to "take care of it." I lied again and said that him being at the house wasn't bothering me.

I asked John to let me drop out of school. I wanted to work with him and Myron. I saw how people around the way looked up to them and feared them. I wanted that same feeling of respect. Besides, I hated everything about school except for basketball. But that was fading fast. Any kind of future through basketball was a dream.

John answered me like he did every time I asked him if I could drop out and work with him: "No. Your black ass is staying in school."

He believed in my skills on the basketball court more than I did. I couldn't see it. I couldn't see past the neighborhood.

"We gonna have a problem here, Julius?" Coach Wilson asked in his office the following morning.

"Nah," I said. "No problem."

"Then why'd you walk out yesterday?" he asked. "If you did it for attention, or if you wanted somebody to chase after you . . ."

He shook his head.

"That's not gonna work here," he said. "You need to be somewhere else."

I didn't say anything.

"Do you want to be here?" he asked.

I really didn't. I wanted to be out on those corners working with my brothers.

"And by here, I mean school," he said. "This isn't just some place you show up to play basketball. Classes matter with me."

"Honestly," I said. "I just wanna play ball. But I know I have to go to class too."

He looked me over for a while.

"You're smarter than you let on, son," he said. "That's the reason that we brought you up to varsity early. It's not your talent. You're not the most talented by any stretch. It's your smarts. You know the game. You know where your teammates are supposed to be even when they don't know."

I just sat, listening.

"Your smarts show when you're out there on that court."

He waited for me to say something, but I didn't know what to say. I had this different feeling about Coach Wilson, though. I didn't see him as someone to fear anymore.

"How are things at home?" he asked.

I shook my head and looked away from him. I could look him in the eye when he was talking about me, but my home life, my family—those topics caused me to look away.

"I knew your older brother, John," he said. "Did you know that?"

"Yeah, when John was here he played for you, right?"

"He was one of the finest players I ever coached," Coach said. "I had to petition the city to get him eligible to come here because he lived in Anacostia."

I remembered the small, dirty apartment we lived in when John went to Dunbar.

"He was like you," Coach said. "Not flashy. But boy could he help a team win."

I didn't say anything.

"But I lost him," he said. "He dropped out of school senior year."

I didn't know that John dropped out of school early. He never told me that, but it made sense—his rule that I had to finish up at Dunbar.

"And now I feel like I'm losing you too," he said, nodding to the door. "To the streets."

"Nah, I'm with you, Coach."

I said it even though I didn't really believe it.

"Let's make a deal here," he said. "I want you to let me know anytime you start to get that feeling that you wanna give it all up. You can tell me. I won't judge you. I'll just try to help you get through it."

I thought about Coach's offer. Other than John, Coach was the only other person who was real with me.

"Okay," I said. And I meant it.

"And I'll promise you that you will be a big part of the team next year," he said. "If you're here. And if you're committed."

I nodded.

"I'm gonna be hard on you," he said. "And you're

gonna hate me on some days. But I'm only doing it because I expect a lot of you."

"I got you, Coach."

"Deal?"

"Deal," I said.

———

"That's where the bond was formed," Butch said.

"Yeah, I didn't see it then," I said, a little foggy after going through my past.

I didn't look back to the past that much. Even when I was in jail, it was all about the day in front of me. I wouldn't have been able to get through it if I spent my days in that cell going over the past. This experience with Butch was a new one for me. And I learned that day it was going to be exhausting and painful.

"How much more time do we have?" Butch asked as he looked at his watch.

"I actually have a class to teach," I said. "P.E. class."

"Okay," he said with a little frustration in his eyes. "This is fine for today, but we have to pick it up if the article is going to come out on time."

"Okay," I said. "I'll give you some more time on Saturday. Does that work for you?"

"Yeah," he said. "What time and where?"

"There's this basketball clinic that I'm helping out with over at the University of Maryland. We could meet in the gym after it's done. That'd probably be a good place to talk."

NINE

A couple of days later, I went to see Coach in the hospital. I hadn't been in to see him for a few weeks. I always made sure to call the hospital every few days, though.

Coach Wilson didn't look different from when I had last seen him. I was relieved to see that he didn't look worse.

"Julius," he said when I walked into his room.

"Hey Coach."

I took a seat right next to him, like always.

"Are you getting settled in?"

"Things are fine," I said. "There's a lot. But it's coming together."

"That's good."

"How are you feeling, Coach?"

"I don't think they counted on me hanging around this long. I'm feeling alright. I may just hang around a little longer to piss off my insurance company."

That made me smile. Coach had a way of finding humor in sad moments.

"Since you're still here," I said, "want to talk a little shop?"

"Of course."

"It was tough losing Dante to Prep."

"Yeah, that will hurt," he said, shifting his weight in the hospital bed. "The talent level is lower this year. Because I got sick, I didn't get a chance to stock the cupboard for you."

He shook his head.

"I tried talking to Dante several times," he said.

"It's okay, Coach."

"Losing Dante will hurt," he repeated.

"I decided that I'm *going* to run the triangle."

He shook his head.

"That's a risky decision. Its bold, but risky. If the team falters—the finger is going to be pointed right at you."

"That's gonna happen either way, Coach. Anyway, I watched film on every player on the team," I said. "Every second of every game. We don't have one-on-one players. Tremaine, maybe. But he's not consistently creating his own shot. If we try to play that way, we'll get blown out of most games."

Coach didn't say anything.

"But what I do see is a team that can shoot the lights out," I said. "And Patrick, he's a good player, but not the kind of big guy that you can just dump the ball down into. He's gotta be on the move. The triangle will be perfect for this team, specifically Patrick."

He still didn't say anything.

"I just have to get them to play smart," I said. "And to play together."

"It's a hard offense to learn," he finally said.

I could see the fire back in his eyes.

"It'll just be the basics early on," I said. "There's this coach from Boston who's coming down to work with us when we start practicing in a couple of weeks. He knows the triangle and has taught it to high school kids before."

"Just make sure the kids are playing free," he said. "If a kid can't play free out on the court . . . "

Coach was getting tired. He blinked slowly and his eyelids got heavy.

"I don't want to think about the day when I can't find you to talk about basketball," I said.

"Well don't think about it, Julius."

"Get some rest."

I patted him on his hand.

"If I don't get in to see you this weekend, I'll call," I said. "And I'll come in first thing next week."

"Don't worry about me, Julius. I'll be here until I'm not. What you need to worry about is teaching a bunch of high school players the triangle," he smiled wryly. "That's the next trick."

I patted his hand again and his eyes closed tight.

TEN

Butch showed up to Cole Field House a little early and sat up in the stands as I went through defensive drills with twelve- and thirteen-year-old players.

At the end of the last drill, I brought all of the players into a circle and we broke with a loud chant of "Defense!"

I walked over to the bench for some water before heading up into the stands toward Butch.

"Why'd you ask to meet here?"

"Before I went to jail, Maryland was thinking about offering me a scholarship. I was just a junior."

He nodded.

"It's just funny being here, you know?" I said.

"You ready to get into it?" he asked with his notepad and pen ready.

———

Things got better at school and with basketball after that talk with Coach in his office. Things at home got better for a little while too. Anthony wasn't around after he and my mom got into a fight. I didn't see my brothers that much either because I spent most of my time at school.

Coach kept his side of our deal solid. I was the starting point guard on varsity at the beginning of my junior season. I held up my end, too; I focused more at school and became a leader on the team. It felt good to care about something and it felt even better to have responsibility. My grades got better and I wasn't focused on what was happening in my neighborhood. The corner wasn't calling out to me as much. After a while, it stopped calling altogether.

We started the season ten and 0, and I played a big role in the start. I didn't score that much—around ten points a game—but I led the team in assists. I made sure that we were always in the right defense, and if one of my teammates didn't know what to do or where to be, I would tell him. Coach called me his "second coach" on the floor and after a little while he didn't even need to say anything; I knew what he needed from me before he even opened his mouth.

Our biggest game of the season was our eleventh game. If we won that one, we'd have a good chance to go undefeated. The eleventh game of the season was against Ballou, the city champs from the year before. They had beaten us twice—badly—the season before and it was time to prove that we could hang with them.

The game had a little something extra for me because Ballou was the high school that I should've attended. I lived in Anacostia, which is in Ballou's district. The only reason I went to Dunbar is because John wanted me to go there. He wanted me to play for Coach Wilson.

Ballou was also ten and 0.

We were at home. The gym was packed with fans of both teams. There were extra cops in the gym to make sure there was no drama inside. There were also metal detectors to make sure there was no drama after the game.

It felt like the whole city was in the gym ready to watch us ball. I was excited. It was the most excited I had ever been for anything in my life. I looked up in the stands and John was there, way up top as usual, like he was trying to hide. Myron always came to my games and always sat down low.

I looked up to the top of the stands and caught John's eyes. I gave him a nod and patted my heart with a balled-up fist. He nodded back and did the same.

Ballou was a big team and an athletic team who liked to use intimidation. We were a much smaller team, height-wise, but we were a lot faster. We had to use our speed if we were going to have a chance.

Coach brought us up right before the tip and the

buzz inside the gym was hypnotizing. I couldn't hear myself think. Just go out there and ball, *I told myself.* Don't think too much. Let the flow decide.

Our fans were trying to out-cheer Ballou's, but Ballou's fans were known for taking over opponents' gyms—usually around the time that their team took over the action on the court.

This was the biggest night of my life.

Even before the game started, I didn't want it to end.

Coach yelled at the top of his lungs and I didn't hear most of what he had to say.

"Play free! Don't worry about the score!" I did hear him say. "Don't worry about a bad play! Just play free! And take it all in! You'll remember this when you're my age!"

After we broke the huddle, Coach pulled me in close.

"We're here because of you. I wouldn't say it in front of the rest of the guys, but you know it. And I know it. Now lead us!"

"Thanks, Coach," I said, already drenched in sweat.

He patted me on the back.

I joined my team on the court and the ref tossed the ball up in the air.

Our crowd always stayed on its feet until we scored our first bucket. It didn't take long for them to sit down that night. I hit a jumper on our first possession. Just from that first possession, it was easy to see what Ballou's strategy was on defense. They were going to pack the paint and cut off the driving lanes. Basically, they were daring me to shoot jumpers.

I had to calm myself down early in the game. Our crowd created so much energy that it was hard not to get swept up in it. We had a small lead after one quarter. We should have been up more because they didn't shoot well early in the quarter, but after a hot start, we didn't shoot well either and the game was tight.

Coach Wilson gave me a rest at the start of the second quarter. He wanted me to sit close though, because with any Ballou run, I'd be right back in the game. The score stayed close. We took a three-point lead early in the quarter and Ballou answered back, taking a small lead of their own around the midpoint.

I went back in with five minutes left in the half and didn't waste any time getting back into the flow. I hit three more jumpers as they continued to beg me to shoot. Shooting wasn't a strong part of my game; I knew it, my team knew it, and Ballou knew it. I liked to drive to the hole and either finish at the rim or set a teammate up for an easy bucket. Good teams like Ballou take away your strengths to see if you can beat them with your weaknesses.

I finished the first half with twelve points on six jumpers and we led by four at halftime. So far, I was doing a pretty good job of beating them with my weakness.

Coach Wilson didn't say much to the team in the locker room. He was proud of our effort, but the job wasn't done. Ballou was a tough second-half team.

Coach Wilson pulled me aside again before we went back out on the floor.

"I'm not taking you out in the second half unless you're in foul trouble."

"I don't need rest," I said. "I can run for days."

"Keep stepping into that jumper."

The second half started and Ballou hit us in the mouth with a big punch. They started forcing the ball down low to their big men, and they either got easy buckets for themselves, or when we brought the double, open three-pointers for their shooters. Just like that, we were down ten and our crowd was silent. Ballou's fans were trying to take over our gym. Suddenly, we were holding on by a thread.

Coach called a timeout.

"Don't sit!" he yelled to the five of us who were on the floor.

He stepped away from the huddle for a second. He took a deep breath and paced a few steps on the court. The only sounds in the gym were the chanting of Ballou's fans and the jingling of their keys as a symbol of owning the place.

Coach took another deep breath and came back to the huddle.

"I got nothing for you guys," he yelled over Ballou's fans.

It seemed like they were getting louder by the second. We leaned in closer to hear Coach.

"There's no X's and O's for this!" he said as he wiped the sweat off his forehead with his hand. "They're just kickin' our asses!"

He looked at us; his eyes didn't blink. He was sweating like he was out there playing.

"Get back into it!" he said as the buzzer sounded for us to go back out on the floor.

Coach jabbed a thumb at Ballou's direction.

"They're gonna try to end this right now. They've got their feet on our necks. Don't let them break us!"

He gave me a look before we broke the huddle. I had to try and take control of the game. Our offensive weapons weren't playing well because of Ballou's tough defense, and we lost our strong defense from the first half.

Out of the timeout, I forced my way to the basket and scored on a layup plus the foul. That got our crowd up out of their seats and quieted their fans for a second. We traded baskets during the next four possessions and it wasn't until the end of the quarter where we took some momentum from them. It started with me stealing the ball from their all-city point guard and finishing the play with an assist to our shooting guard, Tywon. On the next possession, I deflected another pass and Tywon got the steal. I held the ball for the final shot in the third. I dribbled it down until there were five seconds on the clock. I took it to the left elbow, my favorite spot right inside the three-point line, and rose up for a jumper. The defender hit my hand after I released the ball and the whistle blew. The shot went in. The ref yelled "And one!" Our crowd went crazy. The buzzer sounded for the third quarter to end. I canned the free throw.

Ballou was up one going into the fourth.

We couldn't hear their fans anymore.

I took a seat on the bench and looked into the crowd. Myron was hyped up from our strong third-quarter finish. He was talking shit to Ballou's fans loudly. When I looked up to see John, he was gone. I looked all around to see if he moved to another part of the stands. He was nowhere to be found.

That hurt me. For all his talk about me staying in school and believing in my basketball skills, his actions said something else. I couldn't understand why he wouldn't want to watch his little brother play in the biggest game of his life. Was selling that stuff more important to him? More important than me?

I shook it off with a swipe of a towel over my forehead. I didn't want to lose that game. And now that John was gone, I wanted it even more. Before that moment, the most focused I had ever been was when I was on the corner. I wanted to be out there so bad. I wanted to be feared and respected like my brothers. This feeling I had on the court was different, though. It felt like I was a part of something bigger: something *bigger than the streets of Southeast, something that made me feel like life was worth living.*

I hit three more jumpers to start the fourth. I had twenty-five points—my career high—and there were still five minutes left in the game. Ballou didn't back down either. Any time we took a little lead, they came right back with a run of their own. The score was tied with three minutes to go. Ballou had the ball and called a timeout. We were gassed in the huddle. There were no words—not from Coach, nobody. We just tried to catch our breath. After a little while, the guys were all looking at me in the huddle like I was the one. Usually I looked to set my teammates up, but on that night they were looking to me to score.

We stopped Ballou on the first possession out of the timeout. I took the ball, broke my defender down, got into the paint, and hit Tywon in the corner for an open three. He nailed it. It was his first three of the game and it put us up by three.

Ballou came back with a three of their own. After stopping us on the next possession, they got an easy put-back off an offensive rebound. They were up two with a minute to go. Coach Wilson called a timeout. The gym was almost silent; the fans on both sides looked exhausted from the back-and-forth game, like they were the ones on the floor bustin' their asses.

"Alright," Coach Wilson said as he took a marker and dry erase board. "Let's get into our motion, but quickly. Tywon, you come off two staggers and curl around to the elbow. Julius, if you see him early, let 'em have it. When you get it, Tywon, let it fly. Big guys crash the glass. Now, if they hedge on the screens, I want you to keep it, Julius. We'll have a backside screen-and-roll for you to work off. Either get into the paint or take the fifteen-footer."

Coach looked at us, and then at me. He looked happy, like there was no place on earth he'd rather be.

We broke the huddle and the crowd started up again.

As the buzzer sounded, he pulled me aside one last time.

"You've been killin' them all night with that jumper," he said.

I took the ball and brought it up the floor. Tywon curled around the screens and it played out exactly like Coach said. They hedged and I had to keep the ball. One of our big guys ran up for the backside screen-and-roll and I took the screen. It forced a switch.

Their big guy was out on me, but there was no room to drive because he was giving me space. I had to take the pull-up jumper. There wasn't enough time to do anything else.

I took two more dribbles and set my feet before elevating for the shot.

It hung up there for what seemed like forever.

Splash.

Tie game with thirty-five seconds.

I had thirty points. The first and last thirty point game of my career.

Ballou didn't take a timeout; they raced the ball across midcourt and then slowed it down. They were going to hold it for the last shot.

I stayed tight to my man as he dribbled at the top of the key, running the clock down. Finally, I harassed him into picking up his dribble above the three-point line. He was in trouble. Fifteen seconds were left on the clock. His eyes got real wide, so I knew he was going to pass it to one of his teammates. I tipped the pass with my left hand and the ball went right into Tywon's hands. I put my head down and took off down the floor in the direction of our basket. I didn't see Tywon let the pass go, but I knew he would throw it. I looked up in the air and saw the ball looping to me. It was all in slow motion. It seemed like my life was in slow motion up to that point. I jumped into the air and the ball was right in front of me. A perfect pass. I slammed it with two hands right as the buzzer sounded. I tapped the backboard on the way down.

We won the game. We beat Ballou. We were still undefeated.

It was the best game of my life, and the biggest game of my life.

Little did I know that this game would be the last of my career. I would piss it all away soon after.

"I was there that night," Butch said with a distant look in his eyes. "I remember writing on it. Writing on you."

"Yeah," I said, still rattled.

Butch wrote something down in his notepad.

He looked up to me.

"You know, I didn't put it together right away when I saw you and Josh at Old Ebbitt that day in the summer."

"What?" I asked.

"I remember you clearly now," he said. "You came out of nowhere that year. At the start of the season, Coach Wilson told me that you were going to be a major piece on the team. He *knew* you had something when no one else did."

"A lot of good it did me," I said.

"Yeah," he said. "When it all went down, I was going to write a story about what happened."

"Why didn't you?"

"Coach Wilson."

"What do you mean?" I asked. "Coach Wilson stopped you from writing about what I did?"

"He didn't stop me," he said. "He just asked me not to."

I didn't say anything.

"I didn't really look at it as helping you out. It was more of a favor to Coach Wilson," he said. "You're damn lucky that you had Coach Wilson lookin' out for you."

"Yeah."

I stood up from my chair. Coach Wilson's chair.

"I think that's enough for today," he said. "Let's pick up right here next time."

ELEVEN

After school, I was sitting at my desk going over a practice schedule for the first week when there was a knock at my door.

I looked up and saw Dominique, who had been promoted to head secretary of the athletic department, and she had a look of concern on her face.

"Dominique?" I asked. "Is everything alright?"

"It's one of the players, Coach Crawford," she said. "Tremaine."

I stood up from my desk.

"Is he hurt?"

"No, he's not hurt," she said. "No one's hurt—yet. And it's actually the other way around.

Tremaine was sent out of last period for threatening another student. He's in the main office right now."

She turned around and walked out of my office.

———

I found Tremaine sitting in a chair outside of the principal's office. The rest of the office was empty. His head was down and I remembered the look he held on his face from my own past. It was somewhere in the middle of anger and pain.

Tremaine's look swayed more to the side of anger.

"Tremaine," I said.

He looked up but didn't say anything.

"What happened?"

He shook his head.

"It's okay," I said.

He cracked his knuckles and kept his right fist balled in his left hand.

"Just some bullshit," he said, looking past me. "It ain't no thing. I'm gonna take care of it."

I took a seat next to him.

"Take care of what?"

"You ain't a real coach," he said. "You ain't Coach Wilson."

He was right about me not being Coach Wilson, and it didn't bother me. But I was there. I was there to listen to him.

"I am your coach," I said. "And I want to know what's going on so I can help."

"You don't know me," he said. "You don't know the first thing about me. How the hell you gonna help me?"

"I know that when I talked to Coach Wilson and Josh about you, they didn't say anything about you having trouble staying in class."

He cracked his knuckles again and looked down to the floor, keeping his eyes there.

"This punk ass motherfucker, Deion, he's always talkin' shit, sayin' I got no heart 'cause I ain't out there on the block getting' paid," he said. "I always just ignored that nigga 'cause he a clown, but hearing him say that shit over and over . . . "

"And what happened *today*?"

"He started with that same shit," he said, "talkin' about how I ain't hard."

He lifted his head and looked straight into my eyes.

"What am I supposed to do?" he asked. "Just take it? Today, I finally let him know that he trippin'—that I got people out on the corners too. *You* know that. I say one word to Ty about this nigga Deion and . . . "

I didn't know that Ty was in the game. The night of the Ballou game was the last I heard from him, but it made sense that he went to the streets after his playing days at Dunbar ended. He wasn't the first to have it happen like that, and he would definitely not be the last.

"You feel bad about it?" I asked. "That you're not on the corner?"

"I don't know. Sometimes I be feelin' like I'm weak, you know? For not handling shit like a soldier."

"I know," I said. "I know what you mean."

"That's why I had to put that bitch nigga Deion in his place."

"What did Deion say after you told him all that?"

"Him? He a punk. Once I spoke up, he ain't have much else to say."

"There's a lot of people like him out there," I said. "He's just talking to you because you're doing something with your life. He's just jealous."

I realized then that Tremaine was in the same place I was when Coach Wilson talked to me in his office about my future. The anger, the confusion, the guilt; I knew about all of it. My palms were sweating as I gripped onto the chair's armrest. The room felt hot and I became lightheaded. I knew that moments like these could seem light and easy—but they could be the difference between life and death.

"You aight?" he asked.

I took a deep breath and loosened my tie. The warmth shot from the top of my head down to my toes.

"I'm fine."

"So what do I do?" he asked. "You the coach now—so coach."

"You don't do anything," I said. "That's the hardest part."

———

I told Tremaine to wait for me outside the main office. I would give him a ride home to Anacostia, but had to do something first.

There was a secretary, an older white woman, standing behind the front desk in the office. The desk was about as high as her waist.

"Excuse me," I said. "Can you look up a student's address for me?"

"Sure, Coach Crawford," she said as she typed on a computer keyboard.

I had never met her before, but she knew me.

"What's the name?"

"Umm . . . Deion. That much I know," I said. "And also, he's in the eleventh grade."

"Okay."

She typed some more and then stopped.

"There are four Deions in the eleventh grade."

"Do any live in or near Anacostia?"

"One," she said.

"Okay."

She printed out the address and handed the piece of paper over the desk.

"Thanks," I said.

She smiled and I left the office.

———

Tremaine didn't speak on the car ride before I dropped him off at his apartment. He lived in a small apartment with his mother on one of the streets that I lived on growing up. I knew that part of Anacostia well. I lived in the building right next to his for a little while before moving to another one in another part of Anacostia. This place where Tremaine lived held bad memories for me. It was the first place that I remembered my mother using drugs.

I waited until he walked into his building before pulling away and making my way over to the address I had for Deion.

I didn't know what I was doing, but it felt like something that Coach Wilson would do.

The address was right where I thought it was. It was getting dark and I parked my car across the street from where Deion's house was. It was an old house and it appeared dangerously close to falling apart. I walked to the front door, opened the metal gate, and knocked.

Heavy footsteps approached and the door whined as it opened.

"Yeah?" an old black woman answered.

Her eyes were drawn down and the voice—a voice I knew well—was not welcoming.

"I'm looking for Deion," I said. "Does he live here?"

"You police?"

"No," I said with a shake of my head. "I'm not."

She turned her head back into the house.

"Deion!" she yelled. "Deion! Get your ass down here! Someone at the door for you!"

She turned back to me.

"Wait right here."

She slammed the door shut in my face. I paced in front of it as I waited for him to come.

Deion opened the door and eyed me cautiously.

He was tall and wiry. By the looks of him, he wasn't tough enough to back up the tough talk.

"Deion Payne?" I asked. "Do you have last period with Tremaine Watkins?"

He walked outside and closed the door behind him.

"Yeah," he said. "Who wanna know?"

"Me," I said. "I'm Tremaine's coach."

"Oh yeah," he said. "You that new coach. You did time and shit."

I stepped close.

"Whatever is going on between you and Tremaine," I said. "Needs to stop."

He looked at me cross-eyed.

I looked out to the corner at the end of the block, and there were some kids out there working.

"You're gonna do what you're gonna do," I said. "But you're not gonna bring Tremaine into this. You're not."

He took a step towards *me*.

"I don't really appreciate you coming up into to my house and telling me how things are gonna be," he said before lifting his black hoodie up to reveal the butt of a handgun.

"That's not why I'm here," I said. "I just need you to leave my kid alone."

I couldn't believe *that* word came out of my mouth. I was still a kid.

"Yo, D!" a voice came from the street behind me.

I turned and it was one of the kids from out on the corner.

"You got a problem with this dude?" he asked.

Deion looked past me to the kid on the street. He shook his head.

"Nah," he said. "We're cool. Just havin' a little chat is all."

The kid in the street walked on.

"We're cool," he said, still looking past me.

"What?"

"It's all good," he said. "With me and Tremaine."

I stood there frozen.

"Just tell that nigga to stop talkin' shit," he said.

"Deion, I know how it is out here," I said. "When you're ready. If you're ever ready to come off the corners, come see me. My office is open to you. This ain't the only way to live."

He nodded, and we bumped knuckles. "We'll see," he said thoughtfully. "You know how it is."

TWELVE

I went in to see Coach Wilson the following day after school. When I got to his room, Rose and TJ were there along with Josh. They all had red, wet eyes. Coach's condition had worsened. The room was silent other than the rhythmic beeps of the machines that were hooked up to him. He wasn't asleep. His eyes were half-open, but he wasn't awake either.

"Rose," I said and she gave me a hug. "I'm so sorry."

I extended my hand to TJ and he shook it firmly, just like his dad would.

"Good to see you, Julius," TJ said. "How's it going with the team?"

"We'll see," I said. "First practice is in a couple of days."

He nodded and smiled. It didn't feel right talking or thinking about basketball in this moment.

It was silent as we both looked down at Coach.

"How is he?"

"Not good," TJ said. "His organs are failing."

Rose started to weep and Josh put his arm around her shoulder and walked her out of the room.

"Doctor told us that we should start getting ready," TJ said.

"I . . . "

I couldn't say the words. I knew this was coming for a long time, but I couldn't believe that the time was here.

Coach Wilson shifted in his bed. His eyes focused and immediately fixed on me. He strained and licked his dry lips before forcing a smile.

"Coach," I said in a low, gravelly voice.

"Julius," he said at a whisper. "Sit."

I took a seat next to him and looked up to TJ. He was crying, too, although he tried not to show it. He wiped his eyes and left the room.

"We're not gonna get too many more of these," he said.

"I know, Coach."

"You ready?" he asked.

"For what, Coach?"

"For your first season," he said smiling.

"I'm not even thinking about that right now," I said. "I really don't want to think about that."

"You have to," he said before coughing violently. "Life will go on. For Rose, for TJ. It does no good dwelling on this shit here."

I couldn't speak. My eyes watered.

"Now if you have any questions about basketball," he said, "whether it be on-the-court stuff or managing the team, you better ask it now."

I knew what Coach loved most. Other than his family, it was basketball. If he wanted to talk basketball until it was time for him to take his last breath, considering all he'd done for me, who was I to ignore his wish?

"Well, to tell you truth," I said with a chuckle, "I'm not ready. And I still don't understand why you pushed this."

"With what you've been through, losing a couple of games here or there will be nothing. The more important thing is that you're going to be able to get through to these kids—these kids who come from the same place you come from."

"What can I teach them?" I asked. "I nearly threw it all away. And to be honest with you, I'm not sure if I can hold it together. I mean, there are some days where I feel like it's all gonna go away."

"It's not just you, son."

"Why did you help me?" I asked. "I was an alright player, and I turned my life around for a little while. But then I made that terrible mistake. A mistake that no one should ever make."

Coach looked up at me. He tried to focus his

eyes, but couldn't gather the energy. His eyelids blinked lazily.

"You were the only person who visited me in jail," I said. "My own mother didn't even come see me. Why did you do all that?" Now I was crying.

Coach shifted in his bed again. He tried to sit up straight, but his body wouldn't allow it. It just slumped right back down again. I couldn't help but think how cruel life could be. Coach Wilson was a high-level athlete all the way up until college when his playing days ended. Even before he got sick, he was healthy and strong. Now his full head of black hair was gone and his dark eyes were lifeless, like foggy, faded marbles.

He licked his lips again and fixed his mouth to speak.

"I thought you were going to come in here and ask me my opinion on how to break down a two-three zone," he said, "or how get the kids on the team to focus in class like they do on the floor. That would be easy."

"The last favor," I pleaded, tears streaming down my face. "I need to know why."

"I had to help you," he said.

"What do you mean?"

"What happened to your brother, John," he said. "That stayed with me. And I had to carry it. That burden."

"Everyone knew that John was on *that* track. He was going to do what he did regardless. You or anybody else couldn't stop him."

"That's not what I mean," he said. "Remember how, when you first got to Dunbar, you were screwing up, not listening, not taking care of the things you needed to care of?"

"Yeah."

"And what did I do?"

"You pulled me in close."

"There you go."

"I don't understand."

"Your brother was the same way," he said. "He wasn't the most talented player. But he loved the game. And then there was that other part of it too. The streets called out to him. The streets," he licked his lips, "they pulled at him like a magnet." He paused for a long time, "Nobody was pulling back for John, son."

"That's not your job, though—that's a mother's job. That's a father's job." Tears streamed down my face.

His voice got real quiet. I could barely hear him. It seemed like this conversation was going to kill him; it was as if he was on his last reserve of energy and that after this talk, after he got this off his chest, he would be done.

"That night he was shot," he said in a voice that wasn't really his.

The sickness was ready to take him away. That was the first time I didn't recognize his voice.

I leaned in close to him.

"He phoned me in my office the morning of the Ballou game," he said. "He was shot that night after the game, remember?"

I nodded.

"He called to tell me that there was a war going on in the streets," he said. "Young brothers were dying left and right in Southeast those days. He wanted to tell me that he was probably going to be dead soon, and that he wanted me to look out for you."

I just stared at him.

"I tried to talk him out of it. I tried to get him to go clean, even to go to the cops," he said. "But he couldn't. He was in too deep. All the way, Julius. Beyond the point of no return. Too many young brothers had died out there on those corners because of him. In his mind, this was the only way he was gonna go out."

"He was at the Ballou game that night," I said. "He was up there in the stands, but he left somewhere in the second half."

"He knew he was gonna be dead soon," he said. "He wanted you looked after. That was all he wanted."

"I wanted to be just like him," I said.

Coach shook his head, a single tear rolled down his cheek. "That's why I had to carry it, Julius," he said. "You gotta help these young brothers. For John. I've been carrying that with me since that night. I gotta let it go now."

In that moment, a light turned on. It was like everything that was dark and cloudy became crystal clear. I knew what I had to do. Sure, I was still a young brother myself—barely twenty-one years old—but I had this responsibility. I had to carry it. With all the shit I'd been through in my life—growing up where I did, selling drugs, going to jail—this was the first time I was ever scared. The most important person in my life, the only person who could ever guide me through this, was about to leave.

"You got it inside you, son. Now you got to carry it forward," he said before closing eyes.

His head fell back and hit the pillow with a soft thud. He snored and the sound of his beeping machines again filled the room.

I thought of telling Coach about the situation with Tremaine and Deion, but decided against it. It was time for him to rest.

I stood up and squeezed his hand for what I knew would be the last time. I didn't know what it meant to truly be cared for until I met Coach Wilson. My father was a no-show. My mother was so strung out that she didn't have anything left inside of her to care for me or my brothers. Coach taught me that every man needs something or someone to care about.

"Goodbye, Coach," I said, and I left the room. When I walked down the hallway toward the elevator I felt a step slow, like something heavy was on my back. The truth was, it felt good. I was ready to carry it.

The night my brother got shot suddenly made sense. John just wanted to check his little brother out on the basketball court one last time, but the goddamn streets wouldn't let go of him; the streets wouldn't even let him stay for the whole game.

Maybe if he stayed and saw the way we pulled the win out, saw the way his little brother *led* his team in pulling the win out, things would be different. Maybe he'd still be alive.

That's how strong the pull was. That's how the *life* can fuck you up.

The elevator came and opened. It was empty.

THIRTEEN

Coach Wilson died the next morning with his wife and son by his side.

I got the phone call at seven fifteen while I was on the way to school. Rose said that he died in his sleep, that it was peaceful.

It was one of those sad fall days in D.C. The sky was grey—almost black—and it threatened rain constantly.

The mood inside school was no better. There were sad faces at every turn. The halls were quiet. It was Dunbar's own little funeral for Coach.

Josh was sitting across from my desk when I got into my office for lunch. His eyes were red and raw.

"It's hard," he said. "It's just so damn hard."

And he repeated that phrase or something like it over and over.

Our first official practice of the season was two days later. I didn't know how I was going to get the job done with Coach gone. There were the small details, like my players having no idea that we were going to run the triangle offense. And there were the big things too. Coach Wilson was gone. If this whole thing wasn't real up to this point, it was sure as hell real now.

——

Butch appeared in my office after school. His mood matched everyone else's inside of Dunbar's walls.

"I don't think I can give you anything today," I said.

"I know it's tough," he said. "But today is an important day. Not only for D.C., but for the whole country. He meant a lot to high school basketball in America. You don't know how many times colleges and even pro teams came knocking on this door to get him to make the jump. But he didn't want to leave high school coaching, and he wouldn't leave Dunbar."

Butch paused for a second to catch his breath.

"It was bigger than basketball for him."

"What else can I say?" I asked. "I know all that. You know all that. What can I add to it?"

"On days like this," he said, "emotions are raw. Memories come into focus."

I didn't say anything.

"What do you have up there?" he asked as he jabbed at his temple.

The Ballou game was the high point of my basketball life—my whole life, really.

Next came the low point.

My brother John left the game early because he

had to get out on the streets of D.C. He was a soldier in a war. And like a lot of wars, this one was fought for all the wrong reasons. Young boys like me—soldiers—were dropping left and right. Crews were beefing on a street level. Kingpins like John were stacking guns and bullets and cash to go up against the other kingpins. There was a change coming. Something had to give.

At home after the Ballou game, when the buzz of victory had worn off, my legs were feeling the pain of stomping up and down the court, and my back ached from the burden of carrying the team. Myron appeared in my bedroom in the middle of the night. He shook me violently.

"They got him!" he said. "They shot John!"

"What? John's what?" It felt like a dream. I couldn't see Myron's face, just the glistening liquid falling in lines from his big white eyes. The words didn't make any sense either. The words came between the sobs. "John is dead! He's dead!" I couldn't understand the words. "Motherfuckas killed him."

"Dead? But—but I saw him up in the stands," I said.

"It was that nigga Mo's crew," Myron said between sobs. "They had a bounty on his head."

The words still sounded fuzzy. With John out of the game, Anacostia was up for grabs and the corners were there for the taking.

Myron was ready to die too. He woke me up to tell me about John because there was no one else he could go to. That's what I thought anyway. This wasn't a job for muscle, for someone that you hire. This was a job for family. Myron needed a soldier that was blood. "We need to step up, Ju. This shit is war now."

My mom was asleep on the couch high or drunk—likely both. She had no idea that her first son was shot dead in the streets. She did know that John started selling coke and dope at a young age. She didn't try to stop him like John had stopped me.

To my mom, nothing mattered except the next blast. The night John got shot was just another night for her, just another ride.

I felt the sting of guilt. While John was out there fighting, I was out on a basketball court playing a game. My brother worked the corners for as long as I could remember. That's what male Crawfords did. They made enough money to run corners, and after that, supply corners. I always thought I'd get into the family business too, crawling first as a corner boy, then walking as crew chief, and eventually running as a supplier. That was my dream for the longest time—me and my brothers together in Southeast forever. But John put an end to that when he made me stay in school. Corner boy was as far as I got.

Myron went into his old room and grabbed a few guns that he had stashed away for nights like this. One was a three-eighty and the other two were identical Glocks. Myron used to take me shooting down by the river. He'd tell me the names of the guns and then let me fire them at beer cans and glass bottles. It was a lot of fun. He had to take me shooting behind John's back though. John would've killed him if he knew *that he put a gun in my hands. Guns were the only thing Myron ever taught me about.*

I could see the sadness in Myron's eyes as he wiped and loaded the three-eighty. Sadness and anger. I was angry too, for the first time in a long time. Seeing Myron angry made me angry. It hadn't sunk in yet that John was dead. All I could focus on was Myron sitting there loading his gun, crying. "Fuck these niggas," he shouted. "We gonna kill every last one of these motherfuckas."

I didn't care anymore. I didn't care about school or basketball. Didn't care that I had made some progress. I didn't care about Coach Wilson.

They shot my brother, and where I grew up there was no other choice but to get them back—even if I didn't really know who did it. Someone had to pay. That was the rule around the way, and who was I to break the rules? I was just some little nigga that could play a little ball, nothing special. I wasn't above the rules.

"You comin?" Myron asked as he loaded both the Glocks with hollow points.

"Hell yeah."

I put on a black hoodie. I threw on some jeans and grabbed a skullcap. Myron lit up a blunt in my room. He always did that when he was about to do some dirt. It gave him the courage. I took a couple of hits too. I needed some courage myself.

We walked by our mom on the way out. She was dead asleep on the couch and snoring loud enough to wake up the whole block.

We got into Myron's car and started cruising around with no direction. We finished the blunt and drove some more.

"It was that nigga Mo," Myron said. "I know it."

"You sure?"

"Yeah," he said. "We was beefin' with him over real estate. Dropped a couple of his soldiers and he dropped a couple of ours."

"How come John was out there fightin'?" I asked. "Where was his muscle?"

I wiped the last of the sleep from my eyes. My body was exhausted from the game, but my mind was clear. I knew this night was going to change my life.

"He had a little muscle with him at the game. Fat Ricky was with him," Myron said. "I didn't even see him leave the game. He was supposed to take me with him if Ricky got a call."

"You didn't answer my question!" I said. "Why was John out there fighting?"

"I told him the same shit!" he said as he pulled the car over.

A couple more tears came down from his eyes. He wiped them away with his sleeve and held his forearm over his eyes. He raised his head, gathered up all the shit from his stuffy nose, and hawked it out the window.

"John said he didn't want no more of these little niggas dying out in the streets," he said.

"I bet Mo wasn't out there with a gun," I said. "Fuck Mo!" I shouted.

The anger in my body was so strong that I didn't know what to do with it. I didn't even know who I was mad at. I didn't know Mo from any other nigga in my neighborhood. I grabbed one of the Glocks out of the glove box and stuck it in my hoodie.

"We gotta get him," I said. "For John."

"Any nigga that runs with Mo, too," Myron said. "I don't care if he young or old. Some bodies got to drop."

I looked out of the window to the dark, quiet streets.

"I know you out the game and you in school and shit, but this is family," he said. "We do this and then you and me can run things. We'll run this m'ah fuckin' town."

"Let's go find these niggas," I said.

Myron put the car in drive.

"Mo's gonna be hidin'," he said. "He knows I'm comin' for his ass. But we could definitely hit some of his soldiers, maybe someone higher up."

"Where?"

"There's a show over at The Chop Shop. Should be windin' down soon," he said as he checked his gold watch. "I heard some of Mo's crew is up there with some hos. Lets head over there; wait for the show to end. And when we see them niggas, we spray."

I thought about Myron's idea for a second.

"Nah, fuck that," I said. "Lemme go inside and see who's in there. We don't want to spray into a crowd. That'll get us caught up."

Myron thought as he drove.

"I'll see who's in there," I said. "They don't know me. I haven't been on the corners in a while."

"Yeah, but if they don't know you, how you gonna know them?"

"Tell me what they look like."

Myron laughed.

"Aight, one of 'em, his name is O, he dark, and he got dreads and a long ass nose," he said. "If he's there, he'll most likely be with this nigga named 'Hassan.' He light skin, and tall—like six-five—with cornrows. You can't miss that nigga."

"Who else?"

"If we can hit those two tonight, we good," he said. "And I'll get Mo when he pops his head out of his hole."

We drove in silence for another fifteen minutes

*until we got to The Chop Shop. The club was packed;
you could tell because of all the cars parked on the
street around the building. The club was in a deserted
part of town with only factories and old warehouses
around. The river and Naval Yard were close. John
used to bring me to this part of town to get fried
shrimp, fish, and hushpuppies.*

*You could hear the drums from the go-go band
on stage along with hollers and laughs from everyone
inside.*

*"Aight, go in and scope it out," Myron said as he
stopped the car out in front of the club. "Don't wanna
take the whistle inside. They gonna pat you down."*

I nodded.

"Make sure them niggas don't spot you," he said.

*Myron went into his pocket and took out a fat roll
of bills. He shuffled through the hundreds and fifties
and peeled a twenty off and handed it to me.*

"Here," he said.

"They don't know me," I said.

"That's gonna change little brother," Myron said.

"You and me, we gonna run this from now on. We gonna run D.C. We gonna do that shit for John. We gonna remind every one of these niggas who he was tonight."

We shook hands and I got out of the car. Myron pulled away and parked about a hundred feet from the front entrance of the club.

I walked up to the door and a big bouncer with sunglasses stood in front and patted me down.

"Show's already halfway through," he said.

"It's aight," I said. "I'll catch the rest."

He finished patting me down and nodded at the door. I opened it and walked through. The music was louder than I expected. I had been to go-go shows around the way before, but never at The Chop Shop. There was this skinny nigga standing in front of the doorway to enter the club. Was he one of Mo's guys? *I wondered. He was looking down at his phone and the light from it made his face look twisted. I could see the band playing behind him. It was UCB—"Uncalled for Band." That explained* why it was so packed. Everyone inside was partying it up—dancing, drinking, having a ball.

I walked up to the skinny nigga with the twenty-dollar bill out.

He looked up at me from his phone.

"Nah, you don't need that," he said. "Show's almost through."

He jabbed a thumb toward the stage and went back to his phone. I put the twenty back in my pocket and walked past him.

People were packed wall-to-wall on the dance floor in front of the stage. It wasn't going to be easy to find O. I looked for Hassan instead. There were all kinds of people in there: tall, short, dark, light, skinny, fat. I tried to play it cool like I wasn't in there looking for somebody. A few girls came up to me and started grinding, but I brushed them off. I didn't see O or Hassan. UCB was ready to break into their last song. I knew it because they always ended with that song. I didn't have much time.

I looked back to the bar and saw a few tall niggas.

I pushed my way back there to get a better look. I started at one end of the bar and slowly made my way to the other. When there were too many people in my way, I had to wait to let the path clear up. Near the far end of the bar, I stood there waiting for a path—this couple in front of me was freaking—and there was a tall nigga behind me, with his back to me. When he turned around, I could tell right away from Myron's description that this must be Hassan. My eyes must've jumped a little because he caught my look. His eyes were fucked up, but he didn't recognize me. He just nodded and went back to what he was doing. When the path opened up, I continued down the bar and leaned in close to it. O was standing up against the bar in front of Hassan. He was taking a couple of shots with these two girls.

The song was almost finished. I had to get out of there.

I walked back the way I came. Hassan had his back to me again. He didn't see me leave the club.

I walked over to Myron's car and got in.

"Well?"

"They in there," I said.

"Who?"

"O and that nigga Hassan."

A smile came across his face.

"How many hos they got with them?"

"Two I think," I said. "How you want this to play?"

"How much time is left in the show?"

"It's about to end," I said.

"Aight," he said. "We're gonna park in that alley over there and you're gonna go back over to the club and wait for everyone to come out. I'm gonna wait down by that other alley where all the cars are parked. When you see them come out, follow them."

"What if they aren't parked in that direction?" I asked as I pointed to the alley near all the parked cars.

"Then we can't hit them tonight," he said. "This is the only way."

"Okay, then what?"

"When they come up to the alley, call out to them,"

he said. "Say something like, 'Do I know you?' or 'Hey, what up O?' Something like that. When you get their attention, I'll blast 'em."

"Girls too?"

"They all got to fall, little brother," he said.

I nodded.

He looked back in his rear view.

"They fixin' to come out," he said.

He drove away from The Chop Shop a hundred more feet, and parked in the alley across the street. The alley was empty and open on the other end. It was set up for an easy getaway. Myron grabbed the other Glock from the glovebox and cocked one into the chamber.

"Make sure you're ready to shoot, just in case," he said. "I'll try to get 'em all, but you never know."

I got my Glock ready and put it in my waistband.

We got out of the car and walked back toward The Chop Shop. When we reached the alley next to all the parked cars, Myron jumped into it. He nodded for me to continue toward the club.

"Hurry before them niggas roll out," he said.

I walked down the sidewalk towards the club and there was a crowd out in front. Everyone had smiles on their faces. Everyone was high or drunk or both. The noise that was inside the club had poured outside.

I focused my eyes, looking through the crowd to find O or Hassan. Every time someone tall caught my eye, I had to tell my mind that it wasn't Hassan. When the crowd out front started to clear, a small group of people walked out of the club. Two niggas. Two girls. O and Hassan. I walked a little closer to the club when they stopped out front. O lit up a cigarette. He was swaying a little bit—I could tell he was way past buzzed. The other three just stood around while he enjoyed his smoke.

Part of me wanted them to walk the other way.

The other part of me—that other side, that side that no coach can get up out of you, no teacher can teach how to get it up out of you—wanted revenge. By the time I got out of my own head, O, Hassan, and the two girls started walking my way toward their car. I stood still as they walked past me. They didn't look at me too hard. O looked like he was gone and Hassan had an involved smile on his face as he patted his girl's ass. I followed behind them, thinking of what I was going to say. They didn't buck when they heard my footsteps. To them I was probably just another nigga on the street trying to figure out what to do after the club. We came up on the alley where Myron was waiting. I walked a little faster.

"Yo!" I called out. "You O?"

O stopped walking and so did the other three. He turned around slowly and focused his eyes on me.

"Yeah, who wanna know?" he asked with a clear voice.

That surprised me.

"I just uh . . ." my eyes crept to the alley and I didn't see Myron coming. Didn't hear him either.

"I uh—"

"Well spit it out nig—"

There was thunderclap in my ear and O didn't look like a person anymore. Half of his head was taken off and a pink liquid—a thick, pink liquid—covered his white T-shirt. His body fell to the street with a thud and by the time I looked down, the side of Hassan's head was blown open too. Myron moved his gun to point at one of the girls. He fired and hit her in the chest. She screamed. It was the first sound I heard after the first shot, but I'm almost sure the girls screamed from the start. Her body fell on top of Hassan's and rolled off to the side.

The second girl swiped at Myron with her purse. She hit his hand and he dropped his gun. She ran back toward the club.

"Shoot her Ju!" Myron said as he scrambled to pick his gun up. "Shoot her ass!"

I was frozen. By the time I snapped out of it, she was gone, either back into the club or on another block.

Myron picked his gun up and got into my face.

"What the fuck are you thinking?" he asked. "Why didn't you cap her?"

My mouth was frozen. The sounds of troubled

breathing came from behind us. The first girl was squirming around on the pavement gasping for air. Her legs were kicking at the pavement, at the air, sometimes clipping a long-gone Hassan. The bullet ripped her chest open. Her leather jacket was slick with red paint. It looked thick like mud. My stomach bubbled and I could feel it come up into my throat. She looked at us with huge eyes—I still can't get those eyes out of my head—and a wide-open mouth. I could see the pain written all over her face. Her eyes told us that it wasn't fair, none of it.

Myron walked over to her and shot her in the head. Her body went limp instantly, just like O's and Hassan's.

The street was dead quiet.

I was frozen still.

"Come on, nigga," Myron said, shaking me by both shoulders. "We gotta get up outta here!"

I could see the fear in his eyes. It didn't look like craziness. It didn't look like anger anymore. It looked like fear.

He pulled me in the direction of his car, but I couldn't take my eyes off the three of them lying in the street.

"This is gonna come back on us," Myron said as he started the car. "This shit is gonna come back on us."

———

"And how did you get caught?" Butch asked.

"The girl. The one that got away," I said. "The cops brought her in a few days after the shooting for questioning. She knew Myron and that led them to me. I didn't say anything to the police."

"You didn't put it on Myron?"

I shook my head. "No, but a week later the girl told them the whole story. They booked me for accessory to murder."

"That all?" he asked.

"Yeah."

"And what happened to Myron?"

"He went into hiding," I said. "Right after he

dropped me off from The Chop Shop. In the car was the last time I ever saw him. We didn't say a word to each other on the ride."

Butch didn't say anything. He just wrote it all down in his notepad.

"When I started my sentence, that's when he died," I said.

"He got shot?" Butch asked. "Payback for O and Hassan?"

I chuckled even though nothing was funny.

"Nah," I said. "It wasn't payback. O, Hassan, Mo, none of them had anything to do with John's death. Someone else killed John."

"Who killed Myron?"

I shrugged my shoulders.

"I don't know," I said. "Somebody did. Somebody who was tired of having Myron out there running things. But it doesn't matter who killed him. It doesn't matter who does any of the killing. The streets don't make any sense. That's what it's all about. If you can get it through your head that the streets don't make any sense, everything else in the world will make perfect sense."

Butch studied me for a second and smiled.

"Coach Wilson used to say that about the streets," he said.

"Yeah that's true," I said. "He did say that."

FOURTEEN

I looked my players right in the eyes as they sat down on the bench in front of me. It was right before the first practice of the season. Before we worked on their games—their defense, their jumpers, their free throws—I had something to tell them. This was really the first time that I had the chance to talk to them as a team. Before taking on the challenge of selling them on the triangle offense, I had to do this. They needed to know who I really was. They needed to know why I was picked to replace a legend—the only father figure that most of them had ever known.

I saw confused looks on most of their faces. I

looked to my two best players, my leaders, Tremaine and Patrick.

"I know you guys have heard some things about me," I said. "About my past."

They responded with silence and stares. My assistant coaches were off to the side, allowing me to be alone with the team.

"I just want you to know that whatever it is you heard," I said, "it's true."

Patrick smiled calmly. Tremaine's face was still like always. The rest of the guys looked around at each other in shock.

"I went to jail at the same age most of you are at right now," I said. "I made a mistake and paid for it with part of my life. So, go ahead, ask me about it."

The youngest player on the team, Miles, raised his hand.

"Miles?"

"Is it true you killed somebody?" he asked.

There was silence again.

"Nah, I didn't pull the trigger," I said. "But I was there and that's just as bad. I didn't have the courage to do what I knew was right. I didn't stop it. That may be even worse. I didn't speak up, and that's why I went to jail."

Miles nodded.

"Coach Wilson," I said, taking a deep breath and looking up to the ceiling, "he saved my life. Maybe he did the same for some of you?"

I looked around and could see tears welling up in many of their eyes. I knew behind those tears were stories about times in their lives when Coach picked them up. *Carry it,* I could almost hear him saying.

I knew I would cry if I kept talking about him, so I stopped talking. I didn't want to cry in front of my team before the first practice. Coach Wilson wouldn't approve of that.

"That's it. If you ever have any questions about me, about anything," I said, "just ask. I'll answer."

I looked out to see if there were any raised

hands or eyebrows. There were none of either. My players just stared at me as I stared back at them.

"Okay," I said. "Let's warm up."

―――――

"Bring it up!" I yelled after blowing my whistle. My players jogged to midcourt and formed a circle around me. My assistants stood on the outer edges of the circle. They were all breathing heavy except for Tremaine and Patrick.

"You guys look tired," I said. "We need to get in shape."

The tired ones hung their heads.

I looked around the circle, making eye contact with every single guy.

"We're gonna work on offense," I said. "I know under Coach Wilson you guys ran a lot of random, but that's over with."

There was surprise in their eyes.

"We're gonna run a system," I said. "We're gonna play team ball."

Tremaine put his hands on his hips and shook his head slightly.

Josh entered the gym from the far side. He took a spot on the sideline and watched. I could feel his eyes on me. I could feel everyone's eyes, but I wasn't afraid. I wasn't trying to outrun my past anymore. There wasn't any doubt; this was me.

"We're gonna run the triangle," I said.

Tremaine looked down at the floor. Patrick kept the smile on his face. The rest of my players groaned.

"This is Coach Durant," I said, looking past the players to where he stood on the outer edge of the circle. "He used to coach up north at Boston College. He's going to help us learn the offense."

I smiled.

"And I'm trying to get him to stick around all season. So be cool."

Coach Durant took a step toward me and raised his hand to the team.

"Today we start with the basics," I said.

Patrick raised his hand.

I nodded to him.

"Isn't that the offense that the Chicago Bulls used to run? With MJ and Pippen and Phil Jackson?"

"Yeah," I said. "But you're getting a little ahead of yourself."

The rest of the guys laughed and that lightened the mood in the gym, but Tremaine didn't smile. He couldn't smile and I knew why. He would be *the one* for me, just like John and I were the ones for Coach Wilson.

I looked to Coach Durant.

"Coach Durant, can you come up here?"

He walked through the circle and took a spot right next to me.

"Any words for them before we start?"

"Hey guys," Coach Durant said. "I just want to let you know that this young man standing up here is crazy."

Coach Durant grabbed me by the shoulders.

"This offense is so hard to learn that pro teams don't even try it."

The team was silent again. They realized just how much work they were going to have to do.

"But your coach is a good man," he said. "He believes in you all. If you can learn the triangle, you can exceed everyone's expectations this season. Maybe even your own."

That was the first time someone other than Coach Wilson had called me a man. I had to look up at the ceiling again as he spoke.

"And sometimes a little craziness is good," Coach Durant said with one final smile. "I look forward to working with you and I hope you can come at this with an open mind."

―――――

"No! No! No!" Coach Durant shouted as the guys went through the basic actions of the offense. "When we call center opposite, the two weak-side players stay in their spots. When the action starts strong side, that's when you move!"

As I watched them stumble through learning the triangle offense, I wasn't discouraged. I didn't care that it looked sloppy out there. I also wasn't worried that they wouldn't pick it up. They were basketball players and they were from southeast D.C. Those two facts alone made them some of the most adaptable people on the planet.

My main focus during that first practice was body language. I wanted to see how guys reacted when they messed up. That's when you'd see the fierce eyes and tight mouths not able to cuss—a rule that Coach Wilson made way back, and one that I kept—while learning the triangle. I could see that they were going through a process. If you looked closely, you could see growth. Not a lot of it; that would hopefully come later. First practice was a sign that I had a team that wasn't afraid to work. It made sense too. Coach Wilson had lead many different kinds of teams over the years. He had teams with a bunch of talent. He had others that were workmanlike. And he also had teams that were somewhere in between. The point is that he got something out of every one of his teams. Some went all the way. A couple were historic. All were competitive. The kids on his teams learned something. I had to keep that alive. That's the reason I chose to run the triangle. I had to get the players' attention right from the start. I had to let them know that they were here to learn.

All of the guys seemed to care about picking up the offense, all except one—our most important player second to Patrick.

Tremaine rolled his eyes whenever Coach Durant tried to teach him one of the actions of the offense. He looked awkward like everyone else out there, struggling to understand the point of this old-school, ball-sharing offense. But unlike the other players, Tremaine moped after each mistake.

I had to make a decision on this. This would be important.

When we put the second team out on the floor to go through the offense, the first team came off to watch. I told them that while we were learning the triangle, being off the floor was just as important as being on it. Four of the players from the first team stood on the sideline watching closely as the second unit stumbled through the actions.

One player was not watching.

I walked over to Tremaine as he took a sip of water with his back to the floor.

"Everything okay, Tremaine?" I asked.

"Yeah," he said with his back to me. "I'm good."

"Well hurry up and have some water and get back over there with your team," I said. "You need to be over there with them. The quicker you pick this up, the easier it will be for everyone else."

He turned around slowly. He didn't say anything. He just stared at me with anger in his eyes. I knew the look. It was a look that followed me from childhood all through my time in jail. For the longest time, I couldn't escape that look. It was everywhere: the corners, school, my apartment. At this point in my life, I'd had enough of that look.

I smiled at him and patted him on the shoulder.

"Come on," I said. "Get over there."

The sounds of dribbles and shoes squeaking on the floor filled the gym. I could it hear it all unfolding behind me. It even sounded like there was some progress being made. I heard almost no yelling from Coach Durant.

Tremaine just stood staring at me. He wasn't moving. The kid was testing me.

"Okay," I said. "You go on back. Hit the showers. You're done today."

"What?" he asked with narrowed eyes.

"You go back there and cool off, do whatever you need to do, and when the rest of the team gets in there, we're gonna talk on this," I said. "I'm not mad at you, but I can't have you in here moping around. The other guys look up to you too much for that."

I could see the anger move from his eyes to his

chest. But on the way there, it changed to something more like confusion. He was used to Coach Wilson's loud voice, but I wasn't going to play things that way.

Tremaine turned his back on me and walked toward the locker room. He kicked the door open and the crash of metal settled in the gym, stopping the action on the floor and drawing looks of curiosity from the sideline. When I walked back onto the floor, the action started again.

After ten minutes, I gave the players a water break. I called my assistants up at midcourt.

"What happened with Tremaine?" Coach Durant asked.

"He doesn't want to be here," I said.

"The others are doing the best they can," he said, and the other assistants nodded in agreement. "I think after a week, they'll pick it up okay."

"Yeah," I said.

"Did he get out of line with you?" he asked as he scratched his elbow. "What did he say?"

"He didn't say anything," I said. "But you guys saw him out there. He's the only one not trying."

"That's common," Coach Durant said with a smile. "Especially with the best player on the team."

"I'm not going to let this drag," I said as I put my whistle up to my mouth. "There's no time."

I left the coaches' circle and blew the whistle for practice to continue.

———

After practice, I found Tremaine sitting in front of his locker with his headphones on. His locker was in the far corner away from the rest of the team.

"Tremaine," I yelled.

He turned and took his headphones off.

"Be in my office in ten minutes."

He nodded.

As I walked through the locker room, there was a relaxed mood with the rest of the team. There were smiles too.

Patrick patted me on the back as I walked by.

"Once we get this down," he said with his trademark smile, "teams aren't gonna know what to do. I'm already starting to see the little creases to attack the defense."

"Good," I said. "Make sure you study your playbook. And do your school homework too."

I continued on to my office. We had five more practices before the first game of the season. They would all be important. We needed as many reps as we could get with the new offense.

I got up to my office and it still felt strange sitting in Coach's chair. Everything else was starting to feel normal.

Tremaine knocked and walked into my office. He took his headphones off and sat down in the chair in front of my desk.

"Do we have a problem here?" I asked. "Because if we do, you need to tell me so I can fix it."

"Fix it?" he asked. "Who are you to fix my problems?"

"What's up with Deion?" I asked. "Is he still giving you problems?"

His eyes narrowed.

"I'm your Coach," I said.

"How you gonna bring in this whack-ass offense?" he asked. "I'm tryin' to get a full ride to college and I can't do it with this bullshit."

"I get all that," I said. "But this is the way we're going to play. There are ways for you to shine within the offense. Show the colleges that you can play within an offense. They're gonna like that Tremaine. To be honest, I watched all of your film from last year. You're not a dominant offensive player. Dante took a lot of heat off you, but he's gone now. You got game, though, son. Part of the reason this offense is gonna work is because it fits you. But you need to lean into it."

I don't think he was used to anyone other than Coach Wilson being that honest with him.

"I see you as our defensive catalyst," I said. "You're long. Quick. And not afraid. I also see you as a willing passer and a guy that can knock down an open jumper."

He shook his head.

"On offense though, it has to be a team effort," I said.

He didn't say anything. He just sat there with his arms crossed.

"Either you become a part of *this* team, and work at the offense and play defense like I know you can—"

He uncrossed his arms.

"Or this is as far as we go," I said.

He took a deep breath.

"I'll think on it," he said.

FIFTEEN

Butch sat in my office the next day with his note-pad ready. This would be our last talk before the article was published.

"What's left to talk about?" I asked.

"Jail," he said.

"What about it?"

"Well why do you talk the way you do?"

"What do you mean?"

"You don't use slang, you don't cuss," he said. "It's surprising, you know? You don't sound like someone who grew up where you did."

"I wasn't always like this."

"Then you're telling me the change occurred in jail?"

"Yeah."

"See, that's interesting," he said with a smile.

He scribbled into his notepad.

"Not really," I said. "I read a lot in there. That's really all you're going to do while you're locked up. That and workout."

"A lot of inmates read," he said, "but most don't come out sounding like you do. I'm a reporter. I write for a living and I don't ever sound all proper and shit like you."

I chuckled.

"I talked to your assistants and they all say you're the same way with the team," he said.

"I guess I'm trying to set an example for them."

"So you read, huh?"

"Yeah, there was a book club inside," I said. "Every Monday in the library."

I smiled, thinking on those times.

"And then it got to be so good," I said, "that

we started meeting a couple more times during the week when there was free time."

"You and who else?" he asked. "The others in the book club?"

"Yeah."

"What were they like?" he asked. "The other people in these book clubs?"

"I don't see how this helps your story, Butch."

"Just curious."

"I was definitely the youngest one in there," I said. "The rest of them were older—much older. Lifers."

He wrote that on his notepad.

"The first book we read when I joined was *The Great Gatsby*."

Butch smiled and nodded.

"And these old timers, these lifers, they schooled you?" he asked.

I nodded.

"Here's something for you," I said with a smile as I rubbed my chin. "I read the entire dictionary."

Butch's eyes exploded.

"When?" he asked.

"While I was in there."

"That had to be Coach Wilson's idea," he said.

"That's right," I said.

"See," he said, "that's the number one rule of journalism. Get them talking and in no time you'll have a story."

———

After one week in that place, I didn't know if I would make it. You don't live while you're inside. Your life is put on hold.

They gave me seven to ten years for accessory to first-degree murder. The days were long and the nights were even longer. I had a couple little beefs early on with a few guys on my cellblock. Nothing major. My name rang out because of who I was. In D.C., being John Crawford's little brother meant something.

Growing up where I grew up, you always knew

that jail was a place that you could end up. It's always in the back of your mind. But when the time comes—comes for real—where you're in that little box on top of that hard bed and they walk by, close that door, you hear that clang of metal on metal, and all you see are those bars—that's something else. That's some shit you'll never get used to no matter how hard you are.

Coach Wilson came to see me about two weeks in. He was the only person who even tried to come see me. My mother didn't even put her name on the list.

When I heard that Coach was coming, I thought about not seeing him. I had a lot of shame on me and wasn't sure that I could look him in the face. When it was time to make the choice though, I accepted his visit. Something inside my head told me that I had to stop running. I had to face what was coming, no matter what it was.

Coach sat down in front of me with a sad look in his eyes. I'll never, ever forget that look. There was glass between us. I couldn't even reach out and shake his hand or give him a hug. I could've really used a hug in those early days. "I would've been in sooner," he said, "but this was the first day they allowed it."

His eyes were sad but soft, and there was no judgment in them. The shame washed over me, and it was stronger than I could have ever imagined.

"What happened, son?"

"I don't know, Coach."

I felt like sobbing, but I made sure not to. There were eyes everywhere.

"I don't know," I repeated.

"Myron," he said before putting his head down.

After a few seconds, he lifted it and tried to look me in the eyes, but couldn't.

"He . . . he was shot last night. He died early this morning."

I took the prison phone away from my ear and rested it in my lap.

"This isn't the end," he said.

"I should've listened to you," I said. "I'm not gonna make it. I'm not tough enough."

"You're gonna make it," he said. "I'll help you as best I can, but most of it'll be on you."

"I can't," I said. "There's too much pain."

"You need to get clean," he said. "And I'm not talking drugs or alcohol. You need to clean the poison out of your heart."

"I don't know how to do that."

"I'll help you," he repeated. "But it's gotta come from inside. You have to want to change. And you have to let it go."

"Let what go?"

"All of it," he said. "Your brothers, not having a father, the corners—your whole life up to this point. You have to let it all go. Just let all of that poison leave your body. Start fresh, son—and start right now."

"How, Coach?"

Coach Wilson gripped the phone tight and leaned in close to the glass that separated us.

"It's gonna be hard," he said.

That's not what I wanted to hear him say. I wanted to hear the steps that I could take, but there was none of that.

"But if you really want to change," he said, "you can. And this might even be the place to make that change."

I just stared back at him.

"Tonight, instead of lying in your bed and staring at the ceiling," he said, "pick up a book. Pick a book about something as far away from D.C. as possible."

"Coach."

"Pick something and read it," he said. "Read it with the enthusiasm that you have on the basketball court."

"And then what?"

"Pick something else and do it all over again."

"And that'll help me change?"

The C.O. at the door came over and tapped Coach Wilson on the shoulder. He looked back at him and asked for one more second.

"It will help you change," he said. "You need to see

how big this world is. You need to see that there is so much more out there than the street corners."

The C.O. came back over.

"I'll be in to see you every week, Julius," he said.

I didn't say anything. I couldn't. I just put my head down.

"You take care, hear?" he said.

Coach was about to hang up the phone when I lifted my head up.

"I'm sorry."

"Don't be sorry," he said. "Just pick up a book and go somewhere, some place far away from here."

Coach hung up his phone and stood up. He looked at me one last time before turning around and leaving the visiting room.

———

"Books?" Butch asked. "That's what saved you?"

"No, the books didn't save me," I said. "It was just a step. Like Coach said."

He grunted as he wrote something down.

"Is that all?" I asked. "Are we done?"

"One more thing," he said. "Actually, two more things."

I sighed and shook my head.

"How did you get out so early?" he asked. "After Myron died, did you talk on the murders and get a reduced sentence?"

"No," I said. "They knew all along that Myron did the shooting. They just couldn't prove it. That's why I was charged with accessory to."

"So how did you get out in two-and-a-half years on a seven-year sentence?"

"Coach Wilson," I said.

"Coach Wilson got you out early?" he asked. "How?"

"I'm not gonna give you everything, Butch," I said. "You gotta dig around town for that one."

He smiled again as he wrote.

"You were able to let it go?" he asked, stopping his pen.

He looked up at me before saying it.

"The poison?"

"Yeah," I said. "It started with forgiving myself—then it was easy."

"Okay," he said as he scribbled again.

"What else?" I asked. "You said you had two more questions. What's the second one?"

He looked up at me and a wide smile cracked onto his face.

"What's the deal with this triangle offense thing? It's a joke, right?"

"No joke. That'll be our offense."

"Where did you get that bright idea?"

"When I was in jail, I read Phil Jackson's book, the first one, where he talks about the early Bulls teams. There was this part where he talked about it being tough getting the players to buy into to the triangle."

"And that made you think you could teach the triangle offense to high school kids, kids growing up in the era of individual stats and isolation basketball? Kids growing up on the streets?"

"The offense isn't hard to learn."

"This is a joke, right?"

"No joke, Butch," I said. "After I read Phil Jackson's book, I asked Coach Wilson to get me every book on the triangle offense. And he did. When these kids master the triangle, they're gonna start seeing things about themselves. Great things. They're going to prove a lot to themselves and it's going to build confidence. Brotherhood."

He scribbled.

"You are a real piece of work, Crawford," he said.

I stood up from my chair.

"Now is *that* it?" I asked. "You have enough. I hope the rest of our conversations from this point on are going to be about the results of our games."

He checked his watch.

"Yeah. I know we have to stop for today."

He stood up from his chair and I walked him to the door.

"I'll start writing the piece," he said. "It should

be done in a few days. You'll get the first read. If you have any changes, I'll make them before it goes to print."

"No changes," I said. "However you write it, that's how it's gonna be."

"Okay."

He started out the door and then turned around.

"I gotta hear more about this triangle thing," he said. "Let's meet one more time and I'll add the stuff in last-minute."

"No more meetings," I said, pushing him out the door. "Here it is. I have two reasons for going with the triangle offense. One, we don't have a star player, so we need to have a system."

"But the triangle only works with a star. MJ, Kobe . . . " he said.

"We need a system," I said. "There's no question about it."

"And the second reason?"

"I look at these kids and where they come from," I said. "And the only time they work together, I mean, really work together, is when they're out on those corners. And you know what? They *work* those corners. Out there, they are organized, precise, inventive, and loyal. I want to bring all that onto the court."

He stared at me.

"I just want to teach my guys that they can work together on something. Something else," I said. "That's all."

He smiled one last time.

We shook hands and he left my office. I sighed deeply, knowing that I didn't have to talk to Butch anymore about the article. I could just focus on my team. I looked down at my watch. School was just about to end.

Tremaine would be in soon.

I changed out of my suit and into my practice clothes.

I sat behind my desk and waited.

SIXTEEN

The next day, Tremaine knocked and entered my office before practice. He wasn't nervous or tense. I actually saw the opposite on his face, like he was at peace.

He took a seat in front of me again and kept his eyes on my face.

I waited for him to speak, but it looked like he was waiting for me.

"It's not that I think it has to be smooth at all times," I said. "There will be bumps."

"Nah," he said. "Ain't nothing smooth about this life."

"I just need to know that you're with me. If

you're with me, I will have your back in every way, Tremaine."

"Yeah I'm with you, Coach," he said.

I checked the clock on the wall and it was almost time for practice.

I smiled. "That's great. But you didn't answer my question yesterday," I continued. "What happened with Deion?"

"Aw, that nigga," he said. "He a punk. I was just too fierce for him. He's been backing off. Don't wanna fuck with—I mean, he don't want none of this."

I didn't say anything about my trip to Deion's house. I let Tremaine have that one.

"Okay," I said. "Practice starts soon."

"Aight," he said, getting up from the chair. Halfway to the door, he stopped and turned around.

"Hey, Coach?"

"What's up, Tremaine?"

"Coach Wilson ever tell you about letting things go?" he asked. "You know, like the place you grew up in and your past and shit like that?"

"Yeah," I said. "No doubt."

He cracked a smile for the first time since I met him.

"Coach Wilson," he said. "Damn, I'm gonna miss him."

"Yeah, me too," I said.

"Aight, Coach," he said. "I'll see you out there."

———

Coach Durant was yelling instructions to the first team out on the floor. Tremaine ran with the first team. They were running through the basic actions of the triangle and although it still looked rough, it was a little bit better than the day before. They were getting it.

Tremaine finished the sequence with a layup off a weak-side center opposite action. I blew my whistle.

"Yes!" I yelled.

"Yes!" Coach Durant yelled. "Just like that!"

I blew my whistle again.

"Okay!" I yelled. "Time for a scrimmage. First team verses the second. Both sides, make sure you work the offense! Only four more practices before it's real."

My voice echoed all around us and it was then that I realized that I was the only one who spoke and that all eyes were on me.

"Let's go," I said.

The scrimmage started and the action on the court looked pretty ragged. The players on both sides were thinking too much.

I blew the whistle one last time.

"Stop the time for a second!" I yelled.

The clock on the scoreboard paused. All ten players on the court looked over at me on the sideline.

"You guys need to react!" I said. "There's too much thinking going on out there. It's a simple game!"

"The offense ain't simple," Tremaine yelled. "We have to think about it."

I didn't want to tell them *not* to think.

"Some thinking is fine," I said, "but don't cover up your instincts in the process."

The ten players nodded at me and the scrimmage started back up.

Coach Durant walked over and stood next to me as we looked on.

The first team had the ball on offense and was setting up the triangle on the strong side of the floor.

"Moment of truth," Coach Durant said, hands on his knees, leaning side to side, wincing.

Patrick got the ball at the point of the triangle— up around the elbow. The dribble handoff would be wide open if Tremaine saw it. But actually, it wasn't about "seeing it" at all. Tremaine had to feel it. The triangle is all about feel. There are no plays, just actions.

Something told Tremaine to shift from his spot in the corner and circle around to Patrick in the high post for the dribble handoff. After it happened, Tremaine had an easy drive to the basket for a two-handed slam. Coach Durant jumped into the air.

Tremaine felt it.

"I see you Tremaine!" Coach Durant yelled. "I see you, boy!"

Patrick slapped five with Tremaine and they *both* ran back on defense with smiles on their faces. That's what it would take. There would be many mistakes along the way, but it didn't matter. Little by little, day by day, practice by practice, it would come.

Coach Durant looked over to me. I looked back smiling with my whistle lodged in my mouth.

"This is a work in progress," he said. "But that doesn't meant it can't be beautiful at times."

I nodded.

I thought on Coach Wilson one last time. I got caught up in my own head for a moment and lost track of time.

Coach Durant knocked into me and I looked up

at the scoreboard to realize that I had missed a few minutes of the scrimmage. It was okay, though. Coach Wilson would've understood. *I* was still a work in progress.